Remember Love

Remember Love

stories by
Jody Lisberger

Fleur-de-Lis Press
Spalding University
Louisville, Kentucky
2008

Some of the stories in this collection were originally published, in sometimes slightly different form, as follows: "Bush Beating" in *Confrontation* (Spring/ Summer 2001) and *The Way We Knew It* (Fiction Anthology published by Vermont College/Union Institute & University 2006), "Don't Let the Bastards Grind You Down" in *The Louisville Review* (Fall 2001), "Crucible" in *Michigan Quarterly Review* (Winter 2002), "Point of Distraction" in *Thema* (Fall 2002), and "In the Mercy of Water" in *Fugue* (Summer 2005). "In the Mercy of Water" also won 3rd prize in the *American Literary Review* 2003 Fiction Contest and was a finalist in the *Quarterly West* 2004 Fiction Contest.

Printed in the United States of America
First Printing

Library of Congress Cataloging-in Publication Data

Lisberger, Jody
Remember Love
1. Title
Library of Congress Control Number: 2007939874

ISBN: 978-0-9773861-3-9

Jacket art and cover design by Michael Yefko
Interior design and composition by Kim Stinson-Hawn
Printing by Thomson-Shore of Dexter, MI
The text of this book is set in Janson.

Fleur-de-Lis Press of *The Louisville Review*
Spalding University
851 S. Fourth St.
Louisville, KY 40203
502.585.9911, ext. 2777

louisvillereview@spalding.edu   www.louisvillereview.org

For Jess and Herrick

CONTENTS

Crucible

The emptiness of the stage surprises Sheila. One small bed in the center. One small mullioned window (no curtains) on the far left wall. One wooden door on the right. Other than that, nothing. No broad-shaded lamp to cast warm light over puffed-up pillows. No stuffed chair to cozy into. No carpet. No hearth for a fire. Just the wooden post bed, a small braided throw rug on the pine floor, and—Sheila notices only now—a man kneeling, completely still, his head bowed over a girl lying comatose on the bed.

Sheila counts the already crowded rows as she walks down the aisle. "Sit here," she says to Tom, five rows from the front. Where Julia won't be able see their faces. Won't be distracted, Sheila assumes as she spreads her wool coat over the wooden seatback and settles herself to study the program. She feels the jitters in her hands. Tom leans over to slip a bouquet of chrysanthemums and irises under his seat. "Don't step on them," he says. Sheila nods, concealing her momentary wince. She could say something in response—How could I? Why would I?—but there's no point in discussing anything here. She stares at the open stage—so daring for a high school to keep the front curtain open—then focuses on her program. Julia's name appears in boldface near the top.

"I'll enter near the beginning," Julia has told them with utter calm, as if "enter" were a word she's used all her life. She's offered no other details about her role, only smiled coyly at her parents' questions. Sheila takes a deep breath. Since her daughter's youngest days, Julia has flashed that smile, not as invitation but as warning. As if she were born knowing secrets she would never tell. Only now, Sheila really wants to know: What does Julia know?

Sheila has little time to ponder, for the houselights go down and the stage lights come up as a black girl made to look like a middle-aged slave walks through the stage door, rousing the man to his feet. He chases her away then comes back to the girl on the bed. Just as he lifts her limp hand and starts to murmur, Julia enters. She's wearing a long tan dress with a pointy white collar and a bodice that buttons down the front to where it meets the thick pleats of a full skirt. Her hair (she must have dyed it auburn this afternoon at a friend's) is pulled back so tightly in a braid, her forehead looks as arched and white as a temple dome. As she walks across the pine floor, her head held high, her shoulders back, her arms long and graceful, Sheila stares. Stunned. Does Julia look older—a premonition of the future—or younger—a picture of unblemished youth? Does she look more real or less real in that costume, her face all made up? All Sheila knows for certain is that the bodice of the dress, tight against the curve of her daughter's new full breasts and narrowed into a slender V at her waist, makes Julia look both more beautiful and more supple. Like a birch tree, Sheila thinks. Not the birches she's seen tonight in the school courtyard, bowed and covered with ice, their thin branches clattering and breaking in the wind. No, Julia's bones will never break like that, Sheila reassures herself, marveling as her daughter walks toward the bewitched girl on the bed and the man hovering.

"*Uncle?*" she says. Her voice hesitant and sweet at the same time, as if she were timid. As if Julia were ever timid. "*Susanna Walcott's here from Doctor Griggs.*"

Sheila holds very still. To her ears, this is Julia's first line ever on stage. She enunciates perfectly. Her voice carries like the purest of bells. My daughter, Sheila thinks. Listen to her. Look at her.

But something's wrong. Julia's mouth is painted heavily red. Her lips protrude even more than in real life. As if someone were taking advantage. Mocking the one feature that has made Julia—and Sheila and Tom, though they don't talk about this—uncomfortable all their lives. Painted to excess, Julia's lips seem to pucker in a knot of petulance and daring. Don't cross me, they say. Or is it, kiss me? This is the shock that hits Sheila the most. Not her fifteen-year-old daughter's surprising sweetness or clear ringing voice, but her lips, her full lips, painted by somebody—who?—to look like an invitation to whoredom. How dare they? As if Julia were chosen to play Abigail Williams not because of her acting talent but because of her lips, her impertinence, her exploitable beauty.

Sheila looks out the corner of her eye at Tom, who stares straight ahead. Like Julia, Tom has large hands with fingers that easily curve and reach, but he keeps them in his lap. Sheila wonders if he will reach up suddenly and touch her thin arm, her elbow poised on the armrest, to acknowledge their shared making of this beautiful child. But he whispers nothing in awe, casts her no glance, keeps his hands to himself, as if she weren't even here beside him. Not so surprising, Sheila thinks. Two weeks ago, they decided they would separate. "Don't even think about whether you'll get divorced," the marriage counselor advised. "Take time to heal yourselves, first."

Tom and Sheila (she can still picture their names scrolled on the wedding matchbooks, encircled by gold-embossed hearts) have decided to wait to tell the news to Julia—or anyone—until the play is over. They've agreed to carry on with their usual routines. Which they've done flawlessly, until Maxwell called this afternoon. Over the last few years, Maxwell, an industrial hygienist, has tested the air in their house for radon. When he called this afternoon around one, Tom—who wasn't supposed to be home (Sheila wasn't supposed to come home, either)—answered the phone.

Crucible

"If your 'thing' with him is over, why does he call?" Tom asked a few minutes after Sheila walked into the house.

"How many times do I need to tell you," she answered calmly. His cheek muscle twitched. He barely looked at her. "I haven't talked to Maxwell in a month."

"Then why does he call?" Tom asked, waving some files in front of her face. "And why are you home—"

"I don't know why he calls," Sheila said softly, still trying to appease him. As the guilty party should, she imagines. "Maybe it's time to check our air," she added playfully. The two weeks had gone by so smoothly, she'd begun to wonder if they would separate, after all.

But Tom's words rush back at her now as she waits for Julia to speak. "Air?" he snapped. "Try dead wood." Then he did something she can hardly believe. He chomped his teeth at her. Two quick snaps. So unlike him. As if he would actually bite her. Take off her nose.

"Speak nothin' of it in the village, Susanna," Julia says harshly.

During the three months of rehearsals, Julia has said nothing about the play. Sheila has tried to stir up conversation. "Do you know what a crucible is?" she asked early on, imagining in her own mind a container. A vessel in the old sense, though she doubts Julia knows this kind of vessel—not the ship, but the shape, the urn, like Keats's Grecian urn, with nymphs and lovers entwined

5

in an endlessly seeking circle. Will this be the crucible they mean for the play? Or will it be the other crucible? A test. A trial. Sheila dimly remembers something about witches and a girl—was it Abigail?—who accuses everyone of conspiring with the devil. There must be a trial in the play, a real trial, she thinks.

Eagerly, she watches every word leave Julia's lips. *"We did dance, Uncle,"* Julia insists. *"But we never conjured spirits!"* Julia's voice rises, more petulant now. The daughter Sheila knows. *"It were sport! Uncle,"* Julia cries out. *"No one was naked! You—"*

Naked? Sheila pauses. She doesn't recollect any nakedness in this play. Surely she would remember nakedness. Why hasn't Julia said something about nakedness?

But what a ridiculous thought, Sheila realizes. Julia will offer nothing. Will say only what's necessary. "Of course, I know what a crucible is, Mom." Rolling her eyes. Get real, Mom. Then not another word about the play, except would they promise, please, swear on it, not to read it in advance. Nothing to prepare Sheila— or Tom, she presumes—for the acting they see. Their protean daughter, master of innocent defiance. *"Not I sir—Tituba and Ruth."* Then deference. *"I will, Uncle."* At least there're flashes of obedience, Sheila tries to reassure herself. Perhaps the play is teaching her daughter something.

But when the adults leave, Julia changes. She screams at the comatose girl. Shakes her furiously. *"Sit up now! It's Abigail. I'll beat you, Betty!"*

Crucible

The girl awakes. Cries for her mother.

"But your mama is dead and buried," Julia castigates her with glee in her voice. Sheila cringes at this laceration, even as she feels pride. Her daughter is brilliant up there.

"I've told your father everything. He knows everything," Julia continues. She digs into the girl with her words, as if she truly believes these threats will shut Betty up, will solve everything.

But Betty won't be quiet.

"You drank blood, Abby! You didn't tell him that!" Betty shrieks. *"You drank a charm to kill John Proctor's wife!"* she screams.

Julia smacks her across the face. *"Shut it! Now shut it!"*

Sheila draws in a quick breath. The swat comes so easily, so naturally. She wants to believe they've had to practice it several times, but she worries. Does the audience think her daughter is truly vicious (*is* she)? Or do they know better? They must. Parents of adolescents. Why, this is the perfect play for adolescents, Sheila is thinking. Let them scream, vent, fill the stage with their anger. I hate you. Leave me alone. Get out of my life. Get a life. Sheila's heart races a little.

But what is this about John Proctor's wife? And Abigail? What has Julia been rehearsing these three months? Sheila wracks her brain as she thinks back to ninth grade English class. Sex in this play? Betrayal? Adultery? Why doesn't she remember these things? She looks into her memory again, searching for hot breath and nervousness, for fingers as prurient on the page as on the body, but she sees only penny loafers, pleated skirts, and garter belts with silver clasps that fell off on the stairs. Clasps which you never, but never, claimed as your own. (They must have known something.) How they tittered when Mrs. Nungazer said, "Wear your rubbers." Or asked, "Which period is it?" But betrayal? Adultery? Sheila thinks of her father on the 6:58 out of New Canaan every morning. Her mother lining up the lunches, four little clusters of liverwurst sandwich next to Mr. Chips and marshmallows in Baggies. Dinner at seven. Daddy just off the train with his briefcase and coat smelling like an old fireplace. "Sheila is a woman today, Father." The blush of heat in that moment. Yes, it rushes back. But what with it? Only silence. Nothing like these girls who cluster on stage now. Or Julia who excoriates them. *"Let either of you breathe a word, or the edge of a word, and I will come to you in the black of some terrible night and I will bring a pointy reckoning that will shudder you."* Julia leans into her words as if she were pressing a hot poker into their flesh. Such daring. Such force. Such cruelty.

Sheila feels her heart race again. Imagine if we talked like that in real life. She thinks back to today at the courthouse, of all things, where she waited to be impaneled for a jury. Dutifully, even nervously, she answered "here" when the court officer called out "Sheila Blanchard." Not even her name, but Tom's. She answered so quickly. "Take a number. Leave all your belongings in the cloak room." She shudders again to think of the silent line of jurors

8

marching into the courtroom. One case about a boy whose ear was bitten off by another boy at a party late one night. No parents around. Thankfully Sheila was called for the other case, a woman in heels suing a man in a thin paisley tie for sexual harassment in the workplace. Wasn't that awfully antiquated, Sheila keeps thinking about the man's pointy tie.

During the second act, Sheila puts the pieces together for sure. John Proctor, a young father, has slept with Abigail, his house servant. This is why Abigail—Sheila is trying hard to make the fictive leap and see her as Abigail—is keen to accuse John's wife, Goody Proctor, of witchcraft and have her sent to prison to be hung. Such a pretty picture, Sheila thinks cynically. A play about adultery. Don't read it beforehand. Come only on the last night. Sheila presses against her seatback until she feels the nubs of her spine flat against the wood. Tom's cheek pulses like a heart.

"*You must tell them it is a fraud,*" Goody Proctor insists when John tells her Abigail has confessed to him: the girls' dancing has nothing to do with witchcraft.

"*I think they must be told—*"

"*Aye, they must, they must.*" John's eyes wander.

"*I would go to Salem now, John—*"

"*I'll think on it.*"

"*You cannot keep it, John.*"

"*I say I will think on it!*" His voice explodes with anger. The audience hushes. He stops. Swallows. Speaks more quietly. *"I am only wondering how may I prove what she told me. She told it to me in a room alone—"*

There is a long pause.

"You were alone with her?"

Tom's cheek pulses fast.

"For a moment, alone, aye."

Tom clasps his hands.

"Why, then, it is not as you told me."

Sheila feels his body stiffen. She knows he might look at her. A brief accusatory glance, if he dares. One look, like this afternoon's. As if he didn't believe her reasons for being there. As if she were lying. Just because Maxwell called out of the blue. *"You're* home early," Tom said. At first, she didn't understand his sarcasm.

"I was lucky," she answered cheerfully, thinking he was tired, even grumpy. Not wanting to go back to his office. A free afternoon. Maybe he wanted that.

"Do as you wish then."

"I was recused," she added, pronouncing the word with relish, just as he'd taught her years ago. Rhymes with refused, he'd said. She even took a little curtsy, as if being recused were yet another item on her list of worthy—

"Woman. I'll not have your suspicion anymore."

—distinctions. Sheila forces herself to complete her thought as John's words ring in her ears. *I'll not have your suspicion——.* She thinks back to her explanation this afternoon. How she tried to soften the moment. "All the middle-aged women. Recused. In one fell swoop," she exclaimed, scything her arm through the air, a little giddy—she realizes now—with her nervousness at finding him there. In the middle of the afternoon. Home.

"*I'll not have it.*"

"Do you want to go to bed?" she asked, surprising even herself.

Tom simply stared at her, dumbfounded. His thin lips pulled tight. Lips she used to circle with her fingers. Tell him how soft the skin was. How she couldn't resist.

But she doesn't touch his lips anymore. Their stiffness warns her. Stay off. Their rigidity tells her what she already knows, how things once supple—muscles, arteries, feelings, love—become hard. Can one undo this calcification, she wonders. Hasn't Maxwell said to her, "Love begets love"? Which is why she's feeling better about Tom in the first place. This is the oddest, most paradoxical thing—that being with another man, even for a short time, could be turning her on again to Tom.

Sheila looks at Tom's face. The sharpness of his jawbone. The fuzz on his ear lobes. Surely he knows she's watching him. Is he thinking about this afternoon, too?

"I need to go back to work," he said, staring at her as if puzzled: who is this woman with wrinkles around her eyes, this stranger in my house asking me to go to bed?

"I need to go back to work," he said again, as if she weren't listening. Didn't ever listen. "I'll pick you up at seven. Right here, I presume." He gestured vaguely toward the living room, the brass lamps, the baby grand piano, the damask sofa, the fireplace. As if these things could speak in ways he could not. His eyes paused on the big windows. Light streaking in. She knew exactly what he was thinking. Why haven't you ever made curtains?

At the end of the second act, two people remain on stage—Mary Warren, one of Abigail's cohorts, and John Proctor, who Sheila suddenly realizes is the ever-so-polite Peter she's been seeing around their house. (How do you do, Mrs. Blanchard. Yes, thank you.) He leans over Mary now, full of menace. *"You will tell the court how that poppet come here and who stuck the needle in!"* he seethes.

Back off a little, Sheila thinks, even as she feels herself invisibly nodding. Yes, tell him the truth.

"I cannot!" Mary cries out.

Peter grabs Mary's arm. Sheila feels her own hands clench.

"Abby'll charge lechery on you!" Mary nearly spits in his face.

For a second Peter freezes. His jaw drops. *"She's told you!"* he says in a gasp of horror the audience shares with him. Sheila, too, draws in her breath.

"I have known it, sir," Mary whispers. She pulls away from him. *"She'll ruin you with it; I know she will."*

12

Sheila holds very still. Maybe she won't, she wants to say. Would Abigail do that? She doesn't dare look at Tom.

Peter's face tightens with pain. *"Good. Then her saintliness is done with,"* he cries out, his voice caught between accusation and self-loathing.

Sheila is surprised to feel herself suddenly relax. Her rib cage softens. Her weight settles in her chair. One loses saintliness. One must. Doesn't he know this?

Peter's eyes narrow. *"Abby and I will slide together into our pit!"* he screams. He grabs Mary's arm again. *"You will tell the court what you know. My wife will never die for me! That goodness will not die for me!"*

"I cannot. I cannot," Mary pleads. She shields her broad white forehead. He yanks her arms away (surely they've practiced this) as he puts his hands around her neck. He throws her to the floor where they wrestle. Their gargantuan shadows winnow in ghoulish distortions against the thick back curtain. *"All our pretense is ripped away,"* John cries in anguish. *"We are only what we always were, but naked now, Aye naked! And the wind, God's icy wind, will blow!"* He rises above her and nearly howls in abjection. Not a soul in the audience moves. Where has this boy learned such emotion? Sheila wants to know. Who has taught him? Or Julia. Where has she learned such beseeching innocence, such scathing damnation, or now, in this new scene in the woods, such seduction as she runs her fingers along John Proctor's chest and neck—yes, think

of him as John, Sheila tells herself—caressing his arms, his face, his ears and lips like a seasoned mistress. In front of everyone, she sways her lithe figure, clothed only in a nightgown, against his gaunt body, pressing her hips into his. Her mouth brushes his flesh. Where have mere fifteen-year-olds learned such amorous ease?

Sheila puts her fingers to her own thick lips, as if to cover them were to cover everything. Please let the front curtain down, she's thinking. Please let it drop and shield these two. My daughter doesn't really know these things. She's acting. It's a play. You're supposed to act. Please, put the curtain down. But the curtain stays open. In an odd way, Sheila is glad. She can't take her eyes off her daughter. She can't stop herself from edging forward on her seat as Julia cries out to Peter, *"It were a fire you walked me through, and all my ignorance was burned away. It were a fire, John, we lay in fire—you burned my ignorance away."*

Sheila closes her eyes, hoping to calm her heart. Say Abigail, she tells herself. Not Julia. Abigail. A girl from another century, eons ago. A girl who surely doesn't know the real meaning of adultery. She says the word now, of course. She's learned her lines. A good girl. A dutiful girl. Sheila trembles as she waits to hear more voices.

"Why are you cold?" Abigail cries out.

Total silence. Sheila imagines John backing off. Shirking. Scared.

Crucible

"My wife goes to trial in the morning, Abigail." He pauses. *"Save yourself. I will prove you for the fraud you are."*

"What will you tell?" Abigail taunts. *"You will confess to fornication? In the court?"* She starts to laugh. Not just a laugh (she's brilliant up there), but a scathing, ripping, shrieking laugh, like a witch, of course.

Sheila opens her eyes. She has to see to believe. To know her daughter will survive this attack. Peter taking Julia by the shoulders and shaking her with all his might. But she grabs him right back and forces him against the lone tree. She leans into him. Burns her words into his face, enunciating perfectly. *"I know you, John—you are this moment singing secret Hallelujahs that your wife will hang!"* For an instant, Julia's eyes flit to the audience.

"You mad, you murderous bitch!" Peter screams. He throws Julia to the floor. Sheila cannot bear to watch. She squeezes her eyes shut, her lips, too. Get up! she thinks.

"Oh, how hard it is when pretense falls!" Abigail screams.

Get up.

"But it falls, it falls!" Abigail shrieks. *"Oh, I will save you tomorrow. From yourself, I will save you."*

When Sheila opens her eyes, only Peter remains on stage, frozen as if in terror, waiting for the single spotlight to click off. When it does, for a few seconds the audience sits in darkness and quiet. Sheila's pulse races. "Did you hear that boy on stage?" she wants to turn to Tom and ask. "His passion? His heart set free?

Her goodness?" For a moment Sheila doesn't even think about Julia—that glint in her eyes, the exaggerated passion (surely it's exaggerated), the quick glance toward the audience. Instead she puts her fingers to her lips and presses, as if this touch can hold back the tumult in her head. *I'll not have your suspicion. My wife will never die for me! I told your father everything. He burned my ignorance away. Speak nothin' of it. Why are you cold?*

The intermission houselights come up long before Sheila's ready. She's still trying to sort out the lines. John's and Abigail's. How can she be pulled toward both? Husband and—but no, not wife. Not even a woman, Sheila hears herself insisting. A girl. A play. The mere coincidence her daughter was cast to stroke a boy's face and ears and lips. Why doesn't she remember adultery in this play? Again Sheila searches her memory. She looks for the word, the concept, the heat that rushes through her veins, now. But she sees only clutter. Like her daughter's room. Where is that word adultery hiding? Again she looks and listens—but all she hears reverberating now is Julia's cackling laugh. *You will confess to fornication?* She must have practiced that word, Sheila imagines. That antiquated word. Surely Rachel Lang, the drama teacher, had to prep her, stop her from stumbling and saying something stupid like fornification instead. Sheila can just hear Rachel insisting. Pronounce each syllable crisply. Four syllables. All words made up of syllables.

"Isn't Julia stupendous?" Stephanie Becker, their neighbor of many years, rushes over and blurts out. "You two must be so proud of her."

Sheila looks up in time to see Tom smile first at Stephanie, then at her, as if this pride were the very secret he and she discussed last night. In bed.

"Why, thank you, Stephanie," he says in polite self-deprecation. "I must confess, we're a bit surprised. I mean, impressed, yes," he corrects himself. Even blushes a little. "Just not fully prepared, I guess," he says with a chuckle. He pats Sheila's knee good-naturedly.

Sheila tips her head in gratitude toward Stephanie. The charade. They're getting so good at it. Sometimes she's not sure where it begins and ends.

"Well, I hope you two celebrate this success."

"Yes, you should," Rachel breaks in, her eyes bright with pleasure. "I want to thank you for working so hard with Julia on her lines—"

Sheila smiles. "You're welcome, but to tell the truth—" she looks to Tom—"we didn't even know her lines. She's done it all—" Sheila takes a big breath—"herself."

"No!" Rachel answers in exaggerated disbelief. "Why that's—"

"Tom!" Dan Wakefield, from Tom's firm (Dan's daughter is in the same homeroom as Julia), reaches around Rachel to shake Tom's hand. "And Sheila!" Dan's voice rings out. Tom and Sheila stand up together and shift into the aisle. "Your daughter is incredible! Goodness! I didn't know you had it in you." He slaps Tom on the back and gives a hearty guffaw.

Tom laughs uncomfortably. He raises his eyebrows once toward Sheila. Dan chuckles. Sheila casts her eyes down.

"But, here, let me get your picture," Martha Bishop, the school photographer says as she lifts Sheila's chin and pushes her closer to Tom. "Face each other a little. Will you? There we go. The proud parents of an adulteress," she nearly trills. "That's a new one. Now smile!" She snaps the picture of Tom and Sheila, not feeding each other cake or even holding hands, Sheila thinks, but grimly aligning themselves for the flash. Slowly the hall empties behind them.

"Do you want to go out and take a breather?" Tom asks quietly. He gestures toward the exit with his open hand.

Sheila pauses. She wishes he would say something else. About pride. Or endurance. Or maybe even love. "No, no. I think I'll stay here," she says. "You go if you want." She makes her voice sound extra gentle, hoping he might decide to stay and sit with her. Perhaps he'll insist, You come, too.

But he doesn't.

Tom waits until the lights flash to return to his seat. In his absence, Sheila decides she will say something to him, no matter.

"Pretty amazing, isn't she?" she whispers after he sits down.

She touches Tom's hand, hoping to get him to touch back. She wonders if he thinks, as she does, that Julia's performance could open things for them.

"Yes," he says, and for a moment looks at her. "She's brilliant, isn't she? Now to see what happens." He withdraws his hand beyond her reach.

For the rest of the play, Sheila tries not to worry about his stolid form beside her. Occasionally, as if by habit, she finds herself leaning closer. His wool jacket prickles her upper arm. She wonders if he will lean back. But he remains perfectly still, his cheek pulsing anew when John screams at Abigail, *"Whore! Whore!"* And when Abigail persists in denying his every accusation. Only when the men of the court bring John onto the stage in chains to talk with Goody Proctor does Tom's cheek soften. Goody Proctor, dressed in her prison clothes, too, insists she cannot make John confess—but she will talk to him. Tom sits forward a little as their conversation begins. Their good friend Giles is dead, Goody Proctor says. Giles has refused to confess. Instead he's demanded the torturers place yet more stones upon his chest. *"More weight,"* Goody Proctor repeats his words. The audience hushes. Sheila shudders. As if there were not weight enough. *"It come to naught that I should forgive you,"* Goody Proctor says to John, *"if you'll not forgive yourself. It is not my soul, John, it is yours."* She puts her hand on John's knee. Lifts his face to meet her gaze. Tears come into

Sheila's eyes. Tears she doesn't dare wipe away. Tom glances for a second at her. He sits back with a quiet sigh. What is he thinking? Sheila wonders, almost not hearing Goody Proctor's next line. *"I have sins of my own to count. It needs a cold wife to prompt lechery."*

Sheila isn't sure she's heard right. What is this?

"I never knew how I should say my love," Goody Proctor presses on. *"It were a cold house I kept!"*

Everything in Sheila suddenly stops. The word *cold* rings through her mind. It stills her like an elixir in her veins. First she feels calm, then heat. Heat nobody can see. A cold house. A cold wife. John's chest heaves in pain. He wants his life, he proclaims to the judge. He will confess.

But signing the paper is not enough. He must be made a public spectacle. No. He will not do this. He crumples his confession. Passionately he kisses his wife before the men lead him away.

"Woman, plead with him!" Reverend Hale exhorts as they all stare into the empty doorway. All except Goody Proctor, who walks alone to the barred window. *"He have his goodness now. God forbid I take it from him!"* she cries out. Sunlight streaks across her prison clothes.

"Do you hear?" Sheila wants to whisper into Tom's ear. To tell him not about coldness. Not yet. But about goodness. *My* goodness, she wants to insist.

***

"I must go find Julia," she says immediately after the curtain call, after the hoots, whistles, and thunderous applause bring huge smiles to Julia's and Peter's faces.

"Let her come find us," Tom says. He leans over to get the bouquet of flowers. Lays it across his lap. "What's the—"

"No," Sheila insists. She knows he'll caution her to be less urgent. Less passionate. Don't be pushy. Keep your distance. But she wants to see Julia. Now. She rises and steps over Tom's legs. She doesn't care how she touches him as she squeezes by. She threads her way through the lackadaisical crowd. She's not actually sure what she's going to say to Julia, but she knows she needs to find her. To see her. Touch her. Hug her. Tell her how brilliant she's been. "The play is amazing. Thank you." Can she say that? What about the glint in Julia's eyes? The relish in her voice? Suppose Julia refuses to hug her back?

When she doesn't find Julia in the lobby, Sheila decides to go backstage. She's never been backstage before, but she knows the dressing rooms are behind those black doors. She imagines the clutter—the inside-out jeans, balled-up socks, satin slips, hairbrushes, punk rock CDs, and teddy bears. A group of girls rushes the other direction in the hallway. They've changed into black sweaters and short black skirts, black tights, and Doc Martens. They've re-done their make-up. Simpler. More flesh-toned, though their lips still shimmer with shades of red.

21

"Have you seen Julia?" Sheila asks. Full of breathless giggles, they point to the door with the silver stars on it. Sheila walks to it quickly, then hesitates. Should she knock? Very lightly, she does. But she wonders. Which stars dress in this room?

She puts her ear to the door. Through the thick metal, she can hear a muffled voice. Or is it voices? Who could be in there with Julia?

Once again she knocks. Silence now.

Maybe I should call her name, Sheila thinks, but she doesn't want to embarrass Julia. Or startle her. (Could she really be in there with Peter?) I'll just peek, she thinks, slowly turning the doorknob and pulling the door ajar, enough to put her eye to the narrow opening. In front of her, a rack of dresses, pinafores, petticoats, and shawls creates a curtain. Behind it, Sheila can see some feet. And hands. She pauses. Waits. Only one person. Peeling off tights. One leg. Then the other. Sheila cannot see the long bent back. Or the graceful arms. But she knows by the soft singing and the shape of the motions that this is her daughter. "Julia," she wants to call out. But again she hesitates. What praise can do justice to Julia's artfulness? What words will suffice? You were marvelous? Amazing? You have incredible passion?

"Julia," she starts to call out, panicked for a second. But she holds back. Julia is standing up, her frail shoulders rising above the clothes rack. She walks softly, as if gliding. At the end of the makeshift curtain, she steps into the open space. Naked, she walks across the floor. Sheila stares. At her daughter's long limbs, her narrow waist, her almost concave belly, the blonde fuzz of her pubic hair, and her breasts, reluctant and uneven, as if they might be tender to touch. Still humming, Julia reaches down to take a purple sarong from the floor. She stands up slowly and wraps herself in the cloth. Sheila holds her breath. No whore here. No adulteress. Not even a witch. Just a girl gathering in her own warmth. Beautiful in her aloneness. There's no way Sheila will call out her name now. Julia would only be angry. Or embarrassed. To be caught in this trance by her mother. Without a sound, Sheila turns the knob and eases the door closed.

"I don't want to go home right away," she tells Tom in the lobby after everyone else has left. Julia has given them hugs, told them how glad she was they were there. "The flowers are beautiful, Daddy. Thank you." She's added them to her stash, kissed him tenderly on the cheek. Sheila's kept her mouth shut. The flowers, from both of them. "What did you think?" Julia whispered to Tom, loud enough for Sheila to hear. "You were great," he said. A red tinge rising in his cheeks. But doubtful Julia's seen his color, Sheila thinks. She turned too quickly. "Thanks, Mom. I hope you liked it," she said. Was it gratitude or nervousness in her daughter's voice? "You were amazing," Sheila said. "Now shall we go home?"

But Julia's not coming home, she's announced. There's a cast party. At Peter's. A whole gang going. "Don't worry, Mom.

His parents are there. We're not going to screw each other. I promise."

"Why don't you want to go home?" Tom asks Sheila as they watch Julia leave in a crowd of friends. It's almost eleven-thirty. They both have work in the morning.

Sheila doesn't know what to say.

"Is it something about Julia?" he asks. He looks at her as if she knows something he doesn't. Something from the dressing room.

Sheila shakes her head. She will never tell him about seeing Julia.

"I want to talk about the play," she says, standing very still, very tall.

Tom eyes her suspiciously. "What about it?" he says. Tiredness fills his voice.

"Well, doesn't it make you think about things?"

"You mean about people who sleep around?" Perhaps Tom intends this as a neutral question, but sarcasm gets the better of him. "I happen to think John deserved to hang, for what it's worth," he adds more softly, as if he realizes he's been too sharp.

Sheila pauses. "That's not what I meant," she says.

"Well then?"

She hesitates. "I mean—what about Goody Proctor's words?"

Tom scrunches up his lips and brow, as if searching in his

memory for something lost long ago. "Which words?" he asks after a time.

Sheila sighs. As she's suspected. He hasn't heard.

"Where she talked about coldness," she says quietly.

He pauses. "Yes, she kept a cold house. That was the problem, wasn't it?" he confirms, but with a slight air of admonishment.

"No, that's not what I was thinking, actually," Sheila says.

"Well, then, what do you mean?" Sheila can hear impatience rising in his voice. She knows he wants to go home. To go to sleep. "Perhaps you mean John's line later on," he adds, quoting perfectly, enunciating each word. *"How may I live without my name?"*

"Yes, that too," Sheila says, knowing what Tom is trying to tell her. His reputation on the line. His name soiled. But she has John's other words burned into her heart. *"I have given you my soul. Leave me my name!"* My name, Sheila is thinking.

Half a mile from their house, Sheila tells Tom to stop. She wants to get out. He balks. Looks alarmed, as if it wouldn't be safe for her out there all alone. "The wind," he says. But she wants to take a walk in the cold, clean air before she comes home.

"Don't worry," she says. "I'll be back in a bit."

He still looks doubtful, even culpable.

"I need to be there tomorrow, remember," she says, though not nicely. "To give Julia the news."

She opens the door and gets out. Her plan is to walk up Shutesbury Hill to see the trees under the full moon. She wants to see the shadows. And the looming silhouettes. She pulls up her coat collar, plants her hands deep in her pockets, and walks to the crest of the hill. The wind burns her ears and brings tears to her eyes. But she stays at the top, gazing at the ice-coated trees that shimmer in the moonlight, their naked limbs and bony fingers pointing in a thousand directions.

Bush Beating

You shouldn't lie about eagles, Agnes thinks.

"So admit it was the hawk," she says. "The red-tailed hawk high in the crook of the dead oak tree. Come on, now. Isn't that what you saw?" Agnes leans forward in her chair, speaking toward her son's ear as if she were pouring a thin stream of water between him and her. Just say it was the hawk, and you'll be free, she wishes.

Philip stays hunched, pushing his lower back into the wooden spindles of the kitchen chair until he can feel each knob. He clamps his teeth and stares into his clasped, chubby hands, fingers interlaced, compressing first one row of knuckles then the other. He thinks about the hard white cartilage that caps each of the bones, how if you chew the end of a chicken bone, the cartilage will pop off and you can suck the marrow. But eagle bones are different. Hollow, his mother once said to him. How else do you think the bird flies?

Philip likes the idea of flying like that. His own body is so heavy.

"Philip." Agnes leans forward again, as if she can coax him by her closeness. As if her warm breath on his newly pocked face will soften his mask. "I said before, and I'll say again, 'We can sit here a very long time, but you aren't leaving until I have an explanation.'"

Agnes pauses a moment, listens for a rustle in the background. "Talk for both of us," her husband David has urged. But Agnes can't do that. At the last minute, even with David standing behind her in the corner, watching, waiting, she can't take on the collective "we."

"Your father says Mrs. McGuire saw you in the meadow," Agnes continues. She lets her eyes flit to the window by the kitchen sink. The lace curtains, the aloe plant on the sill, the light that streaks in across the clean Formica counter. She's determined to sound merely curious, so as not to scare the boy off. She will keep her eyes away from his hands, which he clasps and wrings as if to break his bones. She will say nothing about the coagulated blood. Nothing about the sticks. Nothing about the beatings. She will say simply, sweetly, directly, "What were you doing in the meadow?"

Philip keeps his head down. He listens for his father's footsteps behind him. Not going anywhere, just side to side, this heavy-set man who's come in halfway through his mother's questioning and

taken a place in the corner. Layer by layer, peeled off his wraps—
hat, vest, sweater—and hung them on the brass knob of the back
door. Philip gives a silent snort. He can keep this man waiting a
long time by his silence. Can let this man know there's no keeping
Philip from the meadow, or the schoolyard, or his friends, for that
matter. Philip doesn't care what the police say, or the principal, or
even his mother, though her eyes and soft voice always make him
want to creep back into himself. He runs his index finger over the
bloody scratches on the back of his left hand. He should never
have taken off his gloves, never have let them see him before he
washed. Warm water would have done it. Except Mrs. McGuire
had probably called his mother even before he and Michael got
back, the bitch.

Yes, Mrs. McGuire, David thinks. How odd it is to hear
those words, like some formal proclamation, coming from Agnes's
mouth. Not Peggy, but Mrs. McGuire—he tries to imagine her as
such. She who startled him this morning while he was out raking
the lawn, admiring the oak leaves edged with mid-November
frost.

"What a surprise to see your son up in the meadow just
now," she called from the other side of the big circle in front of
the house.

David recalls how Peggy's arms swung briskly as she
approached. He knows those arms well. Bony in their nakedness.

"Him and Michael Decker. Beating rocks," she continued,

29

stopping directly in front of him, her voice almost a taunt, her eyes scouring his for some kind of answer.

Why are you stopping, now? David wondered. He looked quickly toward the house. The picture window.

"I know they're just boys," she continued, her voice racing a little. "But that poor skinny boy with curly hair whacking Philip on the back of his legs. I thought you might want to know."

Know what? David still wonders as he leans against the kitchen door. That Philip was in the meadow when he should have been home doing chores? (Peggy always says her daughter Megan is such "a dutiful girl.") That Michael was beating Philip? That Peggy was scared? David takes a deep breath and folds his arms over his chest. He wants to grab his son. Shake him. Or her. Agnes. This wife grown baggy over time. Too solicitous of the boy. "That hulk of a boy," the principal said.

David taps his foot in waiting. Agnes still has the Sunday crossword before her on the table. She's twisted her hair up in a clip. The kettle shines on the stove. If only I hadn't hit him, David thinks. Last week, Philip and Michael loitering at the Natick Middle School. The principal. The police. His own son refusing to come inside from the circle when David came home from work. "You can't fucking make me do anything," Philip screamed at the top of his lungs, filling the neighborhood. David went after him. Dragged him across the grass circle, back to the house. But first he slapped him, out there where everyone could see or hear. It amounted to the same. He's never struck anyone before. David shudders at the thought.

"Philip," Agnes says again. "Just tell me what happened and you can go." She begins to roll her plastic pencil between her palms. Her hands scuff like sandpaper. Say anything, she thinks, so long as you're not hurt. She wishes David's words from earlier didn't haunt her.

"Philip's in the meadow," he said when he marched inside. She didn't look up at first.

"What the hell's he doing there?" he said more loudly. She kept working on the crossword. (Peggy McGuire chatting again.)

David came closer. "He's in the meadow with Michael." He nearly spat the name.

Michael. The word brought on its own silence.

"Michael, the whore," he proclaimed, his breath hot on her face.

"I wish you wouldn't call him that," she whispered sharply. She turned to look at him. "I asked you yester—"

"Agnes. Stop denying it. Listen to the kids. That's what they all call him. And you know why. Everybody knows why. We've all seen him on the circle, pressing the girls. We know he sleeps with them. He's Philip's best friend. What do you want me to do, Agnes? Pretend it's okay?"

"Philip," Agnes says a little more insistently. She will try to lead him on, provide an opening. "So you were beating rocks—" she says. She knows those rocks. Knows they can take a beating.

Philip pushes his knuckles. One way. The other.

"And you were running—" She pauses here, watches as he raises his head, bites the corner of his lip. Yes, she knows more than he thinks.

"Why were you running?" she asks. Her eyes stray to the hardened blood on his hand. What *was* Philip doing in the meadow?

So many possibilities. She prefers to ponder the better ones. The lone chestnut tree at the rise of the hill. Did he stand by it, fingering the crenelated bark? The logs over the creek. Did he dip his boot toe there, watch the water swirl? Or did he lie by the rocks, after all, and see the red-tailed hawk? Just this morning at breakfast, she teased, "Go and listen for her call" (surely the large hawk was the female). "She will change your life."

Philip had laughed. Silly mother. Stupid hawk.

You ought not to laugh at things you don't understand, she wants to say. But she can't dwell on laughter right now. David clears his throat, takes a step forward.

"Philip," she urges.

Philip checks his watch. He needs to say something. But what will it be? There's so much she doesn't know. So much she'll never know.

Like the simple scene. Philip lets it play through his mind, considers how he'll tell the story so she'll leave him alone. Which parts he'll add, subtract. Like the eagle. He stupidly came in the door and said right off, "I saw your eagle up in the meadow—torn to shreds, dead." He laughed right in her face (I dare you, Michael said), never expecting her to grab his arm, push him down into a chair, nearly spit into his face. "Don't lie to me when your father is ready to tear *you* to shreds. And don't say it's an eagle when it's not."

He'll have to back off on that one. Say it wasn't an eagle but a hawk. What does he care? He's seen neither. All he has to do is say something believable. And he will, because at one o'clock, in twenty minutes, he's meeting the guys at school to play some ball. No way he's staying home to rake leaves with his father—thirteen years old and raking with your father—they'll snicker, throw him a couple of punches. "Old man gotcha, didn't he?" they'll taunt. Michael will be there.

"What do you want to know?" Philip's voice comes out of a deep place, almost a growl.

"Just tell me what happened." Agnes leans back now, takes a quiet breath.

Philip sifts through the possibilities and picks carefully. "Well, you know," he begins (he can hear his father tapping), "I didn't think it would be much of a problem when Michael came by and asked me if I wanted to go to the meadow." There. Pushed onto Michael. He won't tell her that he and Michael—and Megan

33

McGuire—planned this last week. "I knew I had stuff to do, but Ma, it was early, and you said just this morning how much you like the meadow. I thought I might see the"—he gives in here— "hawk, this once."

Agnes smiles ever so slightly, puts down her pencil, rests her hands on her thighs.

Philip chuckles to himself. She rolls over so easy.

Now for the meadow, he thinks. He wants, needs, to say something catching about the meadow. Something to please her. He closes his eyes and recalls not the mown bristle that dug into his palms, or the huge bare trees that loom around the edge, but the meadow's openness. His breath stopped as his eyes lit on that big open space, flashing not with color but noncolor, not alive but dead. He loved it immediately. Ran to the rocks at the center, to the base of the chestnut tree, and yelled into the endless sky.

"The meadow was beautiful," he says softly, putting his weight on beautiful. "I see what you mean."

Agnes smiles. "Did you go to the tree at the crest of the hill?" she asks a bit timidly so as not to pull the story away from him. She wants him to tell everything, even as David sighs heavily behind them, the breath of a man who feels this is all a ruse. A boy telling tales.

"Ma." Philip is careful to begin with this appeal to her heart. "The chestnuts were still on the ground. Some in their prickly cases, but some real smooth and shiny. You were right, Ma.

Smooth as silk." He moves his thumb in whispering circles along the inside of his fingers to show her.

"Was it cold?" she asks. Her questions will help him. "I mean, was the wind that came over the crest of the hill cold? Could you feel it bite the back of your neck?"

Yes, he could feel the cold press into his body, but not from the air so much as from the ground, near the tree, where the treads of mountain bikes and boot soles—frozen like fossils in the dirt—dug into their backs, their butts, their elbows when the three lay down. The ground was frozen, Ma, and we shivered, he might have said, thinking how he rolled on his side so he could— what would he tell her?—run his gloved fingers along the thin ice teeth lining the frost heaves. Break them off. How he laughed as he held up the studded crystals, letting the sunlight strike them, until Michael insisted, "Take off your gloves, man. That's the only way to do it."

Next to him, Megan lay rigid on her side without a word. Her cheeks were red, her lips quivered with cold.

"Kiss her," Michael coaxed him. "Your lips, man, your tongue." When she opened her mouth, he felt her warmth, but her body stayed stiff, resisting, rolled only part way to him, with Michael there on the other side, watching. Waiting for his turn.

"Yes, it was a little cold, Ma, but not bad." Not bad.

Say it again, he thinks to himself, his own mantra. Not bad. Not bad. Just being. Just doing what boys do, but not being bad like Michael when it was his turn to have Megan back. ("Let me show you how.")

"It was cold, Ma, when I walked over the rise," Philip says. And when I turned back, too—but he will never tell her this, never tell her what he saw or felt. Not Michael fucking Megan, which he didn't see, and might never see, but Michael with his pants down, his cock swollen stiff upright as he struggled at Megan's pants, while Philip's cock rose too, hot and hard against his own fly.

"I found this amazing hornet's nest, Ma," he says, "half of it still clinging to a bramble. Look, here."

He takes from his pocket the finely layered whorled skin of the nest, its mottled dry walls pressed as thin and delicate as handmade paper. Agnes watches closely as his clumsy fingertips paw at the edge and start to peel away the curved layers, so tightly spooned, they don't want to come apart. Philip hands her a piece of the fragile skin. As light as air. Streaked with gray and white. It could be made of mouse hair and thistle, but she knows better.

"Those big thorns got me real bad, Ma." He runs his fingers over the swollen veins. "I guess I wasn't paying attention."

Yes, she knows them, the hedge apple bushes overgrown in clumps beyond the chestnut tree. The thorns fool you. They reach out just below the blossoms, so you can't see them (though she's sure they always see you). Sometimes she runs her fingers along the thorns and the branches. Thorns sharper than pencils. Branches that look bumpy but are perfectly smooth, with a ridge along their backs like an Achilles tendon that stretches skin so taut the light almost comes through. She smiles to herself. But of course the branches aren't translucent like that. They are thick and strong, fanning into thorns and blossoms and leaves. Agnes stretches her fingers outward at the thought. She watches the tendons arch. She can't help but muse and chuckle. In another life, she might be a bird or a tree or a hedge apple bush, her body's branchings already set for that. But Philip isn't ready to hear this. It's too soon—or is it too late?—for him to know that thumbs could be thorns, or arms wings, or voices the unintelligible squeals of birds of prey. He would only laugh.

"Go on, Philip," she says more sternly this time. "But now, tell the truth. Why did you run?"

Philip lowers his head, looks into his lap. Because it hurt, he thinks. Instantly he hears another voice. His mother's. In his own head. What hurt?

The stick on the back of my legs, he thinks. Michael beating me.

But no, that wasn't it. The hurt didn't come from the beating. Or Michael's urging. "Your turn. Her pants. Go ahead." Or even from Megan, though for years he would think, if only she'd rolled over so he could have seen invitation in her eyes. But she lay face down on her jacket, arms straight at her sides, her body shivering under her thin shirt. "C'mon, man," Michael said impatiently. So Philip spread himself on top of her. Would have entered her from

37

behind if he could have or had known how. Humped her like the dogs and cats in the neighborhood. Michael would have been so pleased. But he couldn't do it, couldn't even thrust hard, though often he'd imagined his father doing just this.

"What are you waiting for?" Michael said.

Philip couldn't just lie there, so he rocked his body, soft and wide on hers, pressing his dry lips to her neck, breathing heavy, hearing himself, feeling himself, wishing she'd speak or roll over, not paying attention until she wheeled around and ripped at his fat, pimply face, catching him on the back of his hand, the rake of her fingernails down his soft skin. Above him, she rose and slapped him hard. The coldness made his cheek burn. Michael stood back and laughed, nearly bent over, until she took her windbreaker and whipped it across Michael's face, the zipper pull catching on his mouth, tearing open the corner skin. She ran then, screaming. "You fuckers! You fuckers!" They watched her go, slapping their thighs and laughing at her running like that, her long hair matted across her face.

"We're fuckers!" Michael screamed joyfully, jumping up and down. He grabbed two sticks, one for Philip, one for him, and started beating first the tree, then the rocks, then Philip's legs, yelling at Philip to beat the rocks hard, harder, and to shriek loud, louder, which Philip did, feeling the blood rush to his face as he closed his eyes and pummeled the rocks, imagining they were not flint but flesh—his mother's, his father's, Megan's, Michael's, his own.

"So what will you tell us?" Agnes asks. She sees the momentary wince in Philip's face, chooses her words carefully.

"It's like this," Philip says, raising his head. He knows he has to look at his mother if she's to believe him. "Michael and I went to the meadow. We beat some rocks with sticks and we screamed real loud just for the heck of it. What's wrong with that?" He pauses, sees her nodding slightly. "When Mrs. McGuire came around the bend, we ran because she startled us. Hasn't that ever—"

"Mrs. McGuire said there was more to it than that," David interrupts.

Philip turns his head, glares at his father. "Well, what does dear Mrs. McGuire say we were doing?" He carefully spits out every word, though he nearly stumbles over McGuire.

David hushes immediately.

"According to Mrs. McGuire," Agnes says very quietly, "Michael was beating you with his stick."

Philip lowers his eyes. "So?"

There's a long pause. Agnes holds her breath. She keeps hoping Philip will tell her what she's seen from the picture window is not so bad as it looks. Not David and Peggy McGuire—she can handle that—and not even Michael pushing his lithe body upon the girls, stroking their narrow backs and bottoms more familiarly than she ever remembers having done to her as a girl. But Michael throwing hooks at the boys, stepping closer when the boys back up, enticing them to take him down, pin him to the ground, pummel him. Philip on top of Michael, pressing that boy into the ground. (Didn't he ask for it? Get him to cry Uncle!) How many times has she wanted to march out to the circle and yell at him? Get off. Cut it out. The whole world watching.

"I'm sorry he beat your legs," Agnes says. She reaches toward his knee.

Don't put your hand on the boy's leg, David thinks. He won't like that. He's grown too old for that.

"But you know you have strong legs," Agnes continues. She lays her hand on his knee. "Strong bones, and a strong—"

Philip jerks to one side. Don't talk about my legs or my bones or my body, he thinks. Don't touch me. He clenches his hands together, his knuckles yellow under the skin. He keeps his eyes down. Don't look at me like you trust me, he wants to yell at her, or believe me or love me, because then I'll have to make up something that will really hurt you, like I mauled your stupid hawk, found her at the base of the tree, bloodied by the dogs and almost not breathing. I heard her cry. I stomped on her. I beat her. Beat her. He says the words over and over in his mind, wishing they were true, wishing they would fill him with a sense of power. But they don't. He just feels smaller and smaller. He hasn't heard any goddamn hawk. He hasn't risen up in any meadow. Even the beating on the back of his legs—he wants to reach around and touch there—can't erase the sound of Michael's laughter echoing in his head.

Philip pushes up from his chair. His parents say nothing. He slumps out the back door, grabbing his basketball as he goes.

"You let him get away," David says.

Agnes nods wearily. What is she to say? Something happened up there. But what it was, she can't tell.

"I didn't mean to scare him off," she says genuinely. She looks up at David. For a moment—is it fatigue or desperation that gives her this odd rush of hope?—she wonders, could she and David change things right now?

"Well, you did," David says abruptly. "Congratulations."

"At least I didn't strike him," she says. The words come out faster than she expects.

David's face reddens. He jams his hands into his pockets.

"Sorry," she says, and almost means it. "I was trying to help him. Couldn't you see how he struggled?"

"Yes, well. Boys struggle. That's life."

"Of course they do. And so do girls," she can't help adding.

"Thank you for telling me," David snaps.

Agnes pauses, swallows, waits for the air to clear. She will give it a fresh start. Let him have his say, now.

"So what do you think happened up there?" she asks.

He looks at her. Does she really want to know?

She nods.

"Oh—" He lets the word drift as he scrunches up his face. "Could be anything."

41

"Such as?"

"Oh—" he starts again, as if biding for time. As if whimsy can make this easier. "Could be fire, or tearing down tree limbs and bushes, or beating rocks, or plain old sex. With Michael," he shrugs, "probably all of the above, especially the latter." He shakes his head helplessly.

"You mean with a girl, don't you?" Agnes asks abruptly.

She watches David's face suddenly change registers.

"Jesus," he says. "I can't imagine otherwise."

"Well, did you—as a boy—ever do that?"

"Do what?"

"You know, try things out. With the boys."

David's eyes open wide. Is this Agnes asking? Has he entered someone like that? Been entered? What does she know? He shakes his head, looks her dead-eye in the face and says, No. He's never entered anyone in any way she doesn't already know. Then he smiles. "You know the boy's lying, don't you? He didn't see any eagle, or any hawk. He's made up those stories to please you. Acted the whole thing out. Even the hornets' nest. If he really found that in a bush, I'd be surprised. You know he's lying, don't you?"

Agnes hears him repeat himself and wonders. Does he think I don't listen? Does he think I don't see? She decides in that instant to hold on to Peggy's name for another time. "Of course, I know he's lying," she says. She picks up her pencil, starts rolling it between her palms. "What else did you expect?"

In the Mercy of Water

The first time I see Annabel jump from Simmons Bridge, she looks like a sliver in the air, a splinter of falling light. It isn't just her long legs outstretched, locked at the ankles, toes pointed toward the water that make her look sharp and invincible, or the evening summer sun that lights up the whole side of her body, but her bony arms pressed skyward as if in prayer. Not that she wants us to think she's asking for something. Not Annabel. Never ask. Merely proceed.

Even as she prepares to jump, she makes certain to look as if she were simply responding to Billy's instructions. "Jump way out. Beyond the rocks and the broken branches. See them?" Together they peer over the edge of the railroad bridge, forty feet down into the gorge. Billy keeps a foot on the rail. To feel the vibration, he says. Just in case.

"One last thing," he adds, still out of breath from his own leap. He points to the ragged timbers jutting from the abutment.

"You gotta jump like you mean it. Straight and clean. Yeah?" He touches a hand to her shoulder.

Damn you for listening to him, I want to call out to her. And, damn you, Billy, for telling her to do it. But I only watch as Annabel curls her toes over the edge of the trestle, crouches, and without so much as a glance toward me, thrusts forward her arms and leaps, hollering not "Geronimo" but "Oh shit" as she goes down, a knife into the dark pool.

When she comes up, her laughter is beyond exuberant, almost hysterical.

"What a rush!" she yells to the four of us—me, Jenny, and Betsy standing on the rock ledge, and Billy making his way back from the first opening in the trestle. She must see our eyes fixed on her, mesmerized by her bare scissoring legs, her pale arms sweeping in slow circles.

"Did you go deep?" Billy yells.

What is he thinking? Would she be mightier if she had?

She shakes her head.

"No way!" She cups her hand around her mouth like a megaphone. "Too cold down there!" Her lush Southern accent rings out over the river, so unlike the flatness of our Connecticut voices. She laughs again then strokes toward the bank, proud of her own happiness.

"Anybody else?" Billy looks at each of us. He pauses the longest on me. "You got the nerve this time, Kate?" His voice has a swagger to it. As if to prove my mettle, I have to follow suit. Or is it the reverse? Not my mettle but his he's testing? He keeps his eyes on me as he bunches up his T-shirt and uses it to towel off his chest, flexing his muscles as if he's the next Rocky. And what if I do jump, I wonder. Will I be submitting or rebelling?

"Show him who has the balls," Annabel said earlier. "Jump."

As much as I love Annabel's bravado, I hate Billy's more. "No thanks," I tell him, turning away.

"But Kate," he says, grabbing my arm, pulling me to one side. "Could be a new trio—you, me, and Annabel—big opportunity," he whispers. "C'mon, jump."

I shake my head. Just like last week up at Hound Rock. Only Billy and Annabel jumped then, too. Hand-in-hand in the dark over the sheer rock face. "We'll hoot like hyenas as we go down," they said. But on the bank below, Jenny, Betsy, and I heard nothing until their heads erupted from the black water and their laughter spewed out over the river. In the moonlight, I saw Billy raise Annabel's hand high in the air. Not as if she'd won some strenuous bout, but as if he, by declaring himself her judge, was declaring her his prize, too.

"So, what's the problem this time, Kate?" Billy says. He sweeps his shirt along his muscular arms. He thinks we spend our days admiring his pectorals, his abductors, his biceps brachii—the muscles we learned last year in tenth grade. To a certain extent, he's right. We watch every bulge, every curve, though we aren't about to admit our fascination. We tell each other how much we hate him. Swear he'll never have us. He's our pact, the thing we'll resist together.

Down below, on her belly, Annabel inches along the flat rocks, thick with slime. She pushes aside the foliage on the bank to make her own path, ignoring the trail already there. The thought of her bravado buoys me.

"I'm just in awe of that bulge in your shorts, Billy," I say, loud enough for Jenny and Betsy to hear. I wait for them to laugh, but they don't. They look down at the ground, Jenny with her T-shirt stretched over her hips, a book under her arm. Betsy with her curly hair pulled high in a ponytail, asking again and again, what happens when you hit the water? Does it hurt? As if she would ever jump.

Billy looks down, as if to hide his own blush, before he stares back at me. "You're scared, aren't you," he says. He flashes that boy-beautiful smile.

I could answer all sorts of things. Like this jumping crap doesn't give me a rush the way it does you. I can't be bothered. It's stupid. Leave my friends out of it. Or, yeah, it scares the shit out of me. But admitting fear would be as bad as pretending I don't like sex.

"No," I answer quickly. "I just don't feel like jumping."

Billy smiles and leans close. "If you don't plan to jump, Kate, why do you come? To see me—or her?" He stares at me with his ice blue eyes, eyes that say, I almost had you once. I'll have you again. But even if we kissed and touched in tenth grade, even if he fingered me wet between my legs, *let me touch you*, another of his instructions, he's not going to have me again.

"None of your business," I say.

"Is that so?" he taunts.

Behind us, Annabel parts the brush.

"That was incredible!" she says, breathy and lush. She tilts her head to one side, hitting her ear to clear out the water. She jumps a few times. Her breasts bob. Surely she knows they call attention to themselves. Billy picks up her towel. He goes behind her, draping the towel over her shoulders and rubbing her back. Blood runs down the outside of her calf.

"That blew my mind, Billy," she says, craning her head around. The breeze brings goose bumps to her arms. Her nipples poke through her tank top.

"You're hurt," I say, gesturing toward the blood, expecting her to be grateful.

Without looking, she leans down and brushes her hand over the cut. "Just a stick, Kate," she says. "No big deal."

Billy squats. Fingers the cut. "No big deal, Kate," he says. *Don't make big deals, Kate.* "She'll be fine." *Be fine.* He runs his hand the length of Annabel's body as he stands up. He must see me glare at her. He hooks his hand around her neck.

"You gonna jump now, Kate?" she asks, her voice soft this time.

"No thanks," I say. Without another word, I pull a shirt over my bikini and head home.

When Jenny calls an hour later, I tell her I don't want to talk.

"What's going on?" she asks. I picture her and Betsy sitting at her kitchen table, drinking Cokes and thumbing through the *TV Guide*.

"Betsy there?" I ask.

"Of course," Jenny says.

"That's what I was afraid of." I hang up then call Annabel.

"You coming over tonight?" I try to sound casual, but I can hear the edge in my voice.

Annabel chuckles. "You upset about something, Sugar?" She speaks low and gentle, full of charm.

I take a deep breath. My mother's gone out on her usual Friday night date. Nothing serious, she always says. *Just friends.*

"You coming over, or are your other attachments too pressing?" I say less nicely.

Annabel snickers. "Who'll be there?" she asks, as if she doesn't know I have the place to myself. But still she has to check. She makes no secret about not wanting to be around adults. Her own parents stayed back in Tennessee, as she puts it. Not dead yet, though they might as well be. When she first arrived at our high school in November, she told all of us she'd been on her own for a year and a half. Waitressed in Memphis, trained to be an

EMT in Richmond. After that, an internship in Little Rock as a homicide photographer. "Got tired of wading in blood," she said. "Tired of seeing red. Figured I ought to come north. See what makes you Yankees so yellow." She grinned as she spoke, so full of confidence, nobody doubted a word.

I can still picture her standing in the cafeteria line that first day, running her hand through her bristly hair. I was immediately in awe. A girl who could drive fast and rescue bleeding people. Who lived without her parents. Who wasn't afraid to go where she wanted or do whatever she damn pleased.

In January, she dared me, Jenny, and Betsy to swim with her in the Sound. I never thought she'd do it. But she plunged right in. Clothes and all. Jenny and Betsy helped me pull her out. Annabel, her lips blue, her limbs stiff, laughed with a touch of hysteria all the way home. Jenny and Betsy started saying she was crazy.

On Valentine's Day, she proposed we drive my mother's jeep up the bank behind Kmart. "Just you and me this time," she said. I let her take the wheel. She gunned it up the incline, shrieked with laughter when the jeep bounced down the other side.

"Aren't you ever scared?" I asked.

"Scared?" She spun the jeep around the lot. "Sugar, if I got scared, where would I be now?"

By the time Annabel arrives at my house, a cool breeze has swept away the day's heat. I've gathered fresh mint from the garden and made mint juleps, something Annabel taught me to do last weekend. "Real Southerners put the mint on top," she instructed. "Bury their noses in it while they drink. Like this." Only she pressed her nose not into her drink but into mine. Then she kissed me on the forehead. "C'mon, kiss me back," she said. "Isn't that what you've been wanting all along?"

"Anybody home?" she calls as she throws open the screen door and strides down the hall, checking each room as she passes. When she enters the kitchen, I can smell the vanilla she's dabbed on her wrists. She's wearing my favorite T-shirt. Teal blue, V-neck. She smiles and does a little tada, raising her eyebrows coyly. But I say nothing. Not yet. I need to know first what she's doing with Billy. She must sense that as I hand her a drink and gesture toward the living room. Nothing like our usual laughter, singing to the music, touching. She prances a little as she walks, as if nothing can hurt her. She smiles when she sees the Scrabble game on the coffee table. Without a word, she too settles herself on the sofa, turning inward and crossing her legs tight in front of her. I reach behind the sofa and pull down the blind. Still saying nothing, I open the Scrabble board across our knees and hold out the bag of letters. Grinning as if his wordless duet were her idea, she lifts her glass in a mock toast. I wait for her to drink before I take my own swig, savoring the sweetness that fills my mouth, the cold that numbs my head.

Our letters clack as we play. Her Q-U-I-L-L on the center

pink star. Her smirk. What a draw. But I'm lucky too. An S on top of her quill. My own seven-letter S-C-E-P-T-E-R. Her face tightens up as she leans over the board.

"S-q-u-i-l-l?" she says. "What the hell is that?"

I smile. The moment seems almost too perfect. "Blue, bell-shaped Northern flower," I say, as if I were reading straight from a dictionary. I can hear the edge of triumph in my voice. "One of the first to bloom after the snow melts. In case you didn't know."

Annabel stares at the board. She blows a stream of air through her lips, a long whistle without sound. "So why don't you just out with it?" she says finally, looking up.

I nod, surprised to feel a quiver of pleasure run up my spine. To have her waiting for me, for a change. I take another sip of my drink. The mint presses against my nose. I breathe it in as I glance around the room, at the quilts my mother has hung on the walls where we used to have paintings, at the photos she's lined up on the mantel. Her and me picking apples. Me on the top of Monadnock. Me and Dad kneeling in our tennis whites, holding a trophy between us. "No need to banish this photo," my mother said. "He's still your father."

"So what were you doing with Billy?" I ask, trying to sound calm but firm. I put my glass on the table, my letters next to it.

She smiles as she runs her hand through her hair. "Oh my—" she says in her honeyed voice. "Do I detect a little—"

"Annabel." I stare at her neck, her soft flesh. "Why do you

51

let him put his hands all over you?" I ask.

She pauses and chuckles. "You mean why don't I put my hands all over you? Is that what you want?" She reaches over and plucks the mint from my glass. Tickles it around her lips like a feather.

On the mantel, the Waterbury clock strikes ten.

"Tell me, Kate," she says leaning closer. "You ever been with a boy?" She looks at me with wide eyes, as if she doesn't know already. As if she herself didn't confide last week, "Anybody can turn a girl on. Any fingers will do the same."

"You told me you don't like boys," I say, focusing on the trickles running down the mint juleps, the circle of water around the base of each one. "On a glass table, water doesn't matter," my mother says. "But on wood it stains." I should be getting coasters.

"Is that so?" she says in a taunting singsong. "And when did I tell you that?" She picks up the board and folds it on itself, the letters stuck inside. As she swings her legs around, she tickles her mint on my nose. I grab the sprig and close it in my fist.

"My, my, we are mean tonight, aren't we," she says very softly.

I take a deep breath, determined to push ahead. "Last weekend, the night you told me about your mother, you said—" I pause to get it right, not expecting the lush Southern drawl that comes out of my mouth. "'I—don't—like—boys.'"

"Oh, do that again," Annabel says, grinning. "You do it so—"

"Annabel, stop it," I snap, feeling a blush rise on my face. "You know what you said," I tell her curtly, as if I can erase my blunder. And I know she knows because she cocks her head as if daring me to repeat the story she told me hours after her jump with Billy, when she and I sat alone in the dark on Hound Rock, listening to the water suck down the river. She didn't just leave her house, she said. Her mother kicked her out. Not because of the girls. Oh, no. Her mother never dared speak of the girls. She spoke of Annabel's hair, her clothes, her *sassiness*—Annabel had spit out the word in shrill mimicry of her mother as she stood up and yelled out over the river the words her mother refused. *I'm gay, mother. You hear me?*

We don't raise our voices in this house, Annabel Sue. I can't hear you when you are yelling.

I'm gay, mother! Annabel had turned to the moon, screaming at the top of her lungs. *Can you fucking hear me now?*

"So what do you want me to tell you, Kate?" Annabel asks. For a moment, I wonder if she's going to remind me how I took her hand and stroked it, telling her how sorry I was. As if my mother and I would ever have that conversation. Or my father, who's too busy telling me life goes on like normal. But instead she pushes up from the sofa and walks over to the mantel. Picks up the picture of me and my mother picking apples. "Something about your mother, perhaps?"

I shake my head. No, Annabel, I want to tell her. This isn't about my mother or yours, but about me. My quivering body in your EMT arms.

"Annabel," I say in a warning voice, "You—told—me—you—told—your—mother—you—were—"

"You, you, you, you, you," Annabel says, a glint in her eyes. "You, you, you, you," she says again, a little louder and then again, chanting as she sets the photo back, picks up our glasses, and carries them into the kitchen. She thunks the bag of ice onto the counter, hacks the cubes with the mallet, clinks the spoon as she dissolves the sugar. Then silence. The silence of liquid being poured over slivers of ice. When she re-enters, she holds out our glasses like offerings, the mint wreathed on top. I shake my head. She sets them on the table in the same rings of water.

"I ever tell you about my daddy?" she asks, quiet and nice, as if we were starting over. She sits down, pats the sofa for me to move closer. I don't budge. She leans back and pulls up the blind. "Now where do you suppose my daddy was," she says, "while my mother graced me with her kind words?" She looks out the window as she speaks, as if she can siphon her story from the moon.

"Annabel," I say, full of impatience, "I don't want to hear about your—"

"Milo fields," she says. "You know milo, Kate, don't you? Early-growing Southern crop? Drought resistant—?" She pauses a moment to savor her own mimicry, then reaches out to touch my cheek.

I push her hand away.

"He was looking out over the milo fields," she continues, starting to talk faster, a false cheerfulness in her voice. "He was leaning against the porch pillar," she says, "right next to my mother. Now, wouldn't you think he would say something to comfort his daughter?" She pauses a moment, as if waiting for an answer, but before I can say anything she lets go with a sharp squeal that seems to come from her ears. "But it was my mother who spoke next," she says, her voice getting higher and tauter. "How well I remember her words. *Your daddy's been down to Buddy's Pool Hall. Down there playing with the boys. Now, isn't that nice?*"

Annabel's voice has become so tight and shrill, I want to put my hands over my ears. "Stop it," I want to yell at her. "Enough of your story. What about mine?"

"Annabel, what were you doing with Billy?" I ask one last time.

She reaches out and presses her fingers to my lips, then stands up and goes to the mantel, stares at the picture of me and my father.

"You know, you don't look much like your daddy," she says. Her voice has an odd tremble in it. "Not like me and my daddy," she says, her pitch getting higher and thinner again. "Why, we're spitting images. High forehead. Round chin. Ears that curl like fiddleheads." As she speaks, she touches each of these places on her face. "Why, some people say I'm the son my daddy never had," she says, turning around and starting not only to laugh but to rock back and forth, tears in her eyes, catching her breath, until it isn't laughter at all filling that room but something more like the scream of an engine about to explode.

"Annabel," I shout, hoping the suddenness of my voice jolts her back. Or have Jenny and Betsy been right all along about her craziness?

Slowly she quiets. Wipes her eyes. "Can you believe that?" she says softly, sitting down. "'The son he never had!' Oh, my, my, my." She starts to laugh again. Except this time it isn't shrill but gentle.

"You know what?" she says. She speaks so quietly I have to lean in to hear her. "All those years my mother knew my father was fucking the boys." She shakes her head slowly. "And look who she asked to leave. Now isn't that a pretty picture?" She blows air soundlessly through her lips.

For a moment I sit very still, my eyes cast down. I'm sorry, I want to say. But I can't summon up the words, can't stop myself from thinking, from knowing—in the moment of uncertainty, I've judged her. Just like the rest of them.

"And about Billy?" she says, turning to face me. "People do things for the oddest reasons. You know what I mean?"

She must see my eyes grow wide with alarm.

"Oh, girl," she says suddenly. She takes my hand. "Girl, girl, girl," she says low in her throat. "C'mon. Let's forget the Billy stuff." She points out the window. "Look. The moon's full. We can jump, just the two of us if you want."

I pull my hand back. Does she think we can just forget?

"You can jump with your eyes closed," she whispers.

I try to imagine going over the edge, seeing the water below me, as if it could swallow me. Hide me, at least for a while.

"I'll hold your hand. All the way down," she says more urgently. She tightens her grip.

For a moment, I close my eyes. Will our laughter spew out like hers and Billy's? Do I want that? I take a deep breath. If I don't jump now, will I ever?

"What is it?" she asks.

So much I could tell her. Of my timidity. My fear of heights. My not knowing what's down in the darkness. Any darkness.

I feel her fingertips on my eyelids, light as air. "Sometimes when you jump," she whispers as if she were reading my mind, "it makes everything easier. Just look at me." When I open my eyes, she shrugs, as if to say, "Am I all that bad?"

"So what do I wear?" I whisper.

"Oh, goodie," she says, grinning. "Nothing with girls. That's half the fun."

"Sorry," I say. "I'll wear my bathing suit."

"Okay, then. Who cares?"

***

On the path to Simmons Bridge, I listen to the wind and try to quiet my heart. Next to me, Annabel can't stop prancing. "Step on a crack, you'll break your mother's back," she chants, accenting the word each time she stomps where the shadows cross.

When we come to where the bridge takes off from the land, I walk ahead a few steps and stop. I look down. The water shimmers in the space between the ties. I put one foot on the rail.

"The train doesn't come through till morning," Annabel says.

I look at her and pause.

"Believe me," she says. "It's my life, too." Without another word, she takes my hand and steadies me as we move along the tar-streaked ties. I rest my other hand against the girders as we walk, glad to feel the solidity of the welded joints, the bumps of fused iron circled like numbers on a clock. We walk past several openings in the trusses, far beyond where Annabel jumped the first time. "We want to be where it's deepest," she says. She must see my pinched face, my small worried eyes, so unlike hers.

When we get to the center of the bridge, she helps me take off my T-shirt. Holds onto my sleeves as I pull out my arms. Loops the shirt over my head, uncatching it from my ears. She folds it and sets it on the rail.

"Don't worry," she says, reading my mind. "I'll come back and get the clothes afterwards. Now can you slip off your shorts?"

I do, looking down into the water as it sweeps by the concrete pilings. You can't tell it's pulling hard, but it must be.

"Okay," Annabel says, resting her hand on my shoulder. Does she feel me shaking? She points down into the gorge. "You don't have to jump out far here. Just straight down. Okay?"

I nod, still staring over the edge into the sheen so black and taut it gives the illusion of stillness, of safety.

"But first you have to let go of the truss," she says. Then she chuckles. "But oh-la-la, what a suit to wear!" She runs her finger along my bikini bottom. "It'll wedge so tight between your cheeks, even floss won't pull it out. Won't that be something." She laughs, meaning for me to laugh, too, I'm sure. A moment of distraction. "But wait a sec," she says. One foot at a time, not even needing to hold onto the truss, she slips off her cutoffs and underwear, folds them, and sets them on the rail with my clothes. Slowly she takes off her T-shirt, her breasts pure white in the moonshine, her tuft scanty and almost blonde, nothing like my own.

"Later, Mahvin," she jokes in a mock Yankee accent, as if this were just the beginning. Then she grows serious. "Now remember," she says. "We have to jump at the same time. Because if one person jumps and the other drags—" She points to the wooden beam running along the trestle. "That could do a number on a person. Yes?"

I nod.

"Okay," she says. "Eyes open or closed?"
"Closed," I whisper.

I know now why Billy and Annabel never hooted when they jumped off Hound Rock. Having your heart in your mouth makes it impossible to cry out, the rush so extreme it's a wonder your heart doesn't burst. But standing there on the rail, I don't have time to worry about my heart. At the count of three, together Annabel and I leap off that bridge, holding our hands tight, sucking in our breath, our bodies cleaving the air until we cut into the water, let go our hands, and feel the coldness swallow us. I don't open my eyes. I let the water take me down. I feel it wedge my bottoms and yank my top. My head aches with cold and pressure. Only when I stop going down do I open my eyes, see the blackness everywhere, and begin kicking, pulling to the surface, my lungs exploding so desperately into the air, it takes a few seconds before my hoots ring out over hers.

Love Boundaries

S ix months of waiting!" Anthony's words ring in Carrie's ears
as she stands by the fence at the Santa Cruz airport, ready
for his flight from Pittsburgh via La Paz to cut through the blue
sky. She smiles at how close to the tarmac they let people stand
here in Bolivia. How comfortable she feels in this place, now, she
tells herself, as the plane's blast of hot air, its screeching shift into
reverse, and its wincing brakes announce Anthony's arrival. As
the plane taxis toward the terminal, she wonders if Anthony is
also thinking about their agreement six months ago. Not written
but discussed at length in their last term of college. Her coming
to Bolivia to work with women in the *campo* will only make her
stronger. It will be good for her—and for them.

But "six months of waiting," spoken as if that's all he
did? Surely he was teasing, she tells herself, feeling a jitter of
nervousness. What will it be like having him here with her for two
weeks? But he'll adjust, she assures herself. If anything, this side

trip to Eastern Bolivia, where it's hot like the States in August—how she's missed the heat of summer!—will ease his transition, and hers. Since January, she's been working in southern Bolivia, in Tarija, where it's winter now. Which is why she loves the warmth that enfolds her here, and why, for just a moment, she imagines she could stay on this sidewalk, in this heat, forever.

But when Anthony heads down the airplane stairs, of course she knows better. Her life is moving and so is his—together they believe as they hold each other again. He babbles with excitement. So glad to be here. Terrified his plane would crash over the Andes. Ridiculous to worry about such things. Whose plane crashes? But he was scared, he admits. Those Andes—sharp and endless and covered with ice. Nothing like the Andes he remembers making out of flour and water in elementary school. That backbone you could touch, he says, laughing as he runs his hand down her spine. How does anyone survive down there?

"But here you are, living proof," he whispers into her ear. He pulls her close, tells her he'll go anywhere with her. Anywhere she wants.

Which is good because she's planned a little detour. She doesn't bring it up until they've stayed a day and a night in Santa Cruz, visited the *campesino*, the big outdoor market, and slept at a little *pensión* with a surprise garden just inside the front door, a toucan in the trees. No need to worry him in advance about her little fantasy—to spend a day and night at the *Paraíso Eco Resort*.

Sure the name's a gimmick, she says when she sees the worry in his face, the questioning look in his eyes. What about the real Bolivia? Or the Carrie he said good-bye to in January, the one committed to working with poor women in the *campo*? But it's all very simple, she explains. She misses summer. The one thing her body can't seem to adjust to down here. She needs heat in August. A swimming pool with the sun pressing into her bones. Just for a day. "Can't we go?" she says, surprised to hear the pleading in her voice.

"*No hay problema,*" he says to her relief, grinning as he rolls this new phrase off his tongue. As if he couldn't be happier, he takes her hand, rides the bus with her to the outskirts of the city, and walks up the long dirt driveway to the factory where the resort office is. When at first he's confused, she clarifies. The resort is two hours away, she explains, not bothering to fill in the details about the international company that likely owns the resort *and* the factory. This is only the office, she says, where she and Anthony sit in polished chairs to sign papers, read about the lure of the jungle, and gaze at the huge glossy photos plastered on the walls. An enormous turquoise swimming pool. A dining patio surrounded by palms and torches. A piano bar lit up at night, shimmering in the middle of the pool. But doesn't she find it a little odd to have a fancy resort office in a factory on the outskirts of a city, a resort without even a sign? he asks when they get outside. Is she sure it's for real?

Not to worry, she tells him as they sit on a bench by the office door to wait for the taxi to fetch them. It'll be a long wait, she warns. Welcome to Bolivia.

But he'll get adjusted, she assures herself, even if he didn't like the smell of pig fat in the marketplace yesterday. The pig fat they put in everything, she told him, pointing at the breads the women had stacked on their carts. "*Pan, panconqueso, Tucumán,*" he'd muttered under his breath as they walked, determined to fix those long words in his mind, he said—easier if he pictures them, the ones stacked like plates and the others folded like handkerchiefs. He much prefers the shorter words, he says, like the ones he's practicing now under his breath. "*¿Cuánto?* How much? *¿Dónde?* Where? *Lo siento.* I'm sorry. *Aquí.* Here." She chuckles at his echoing English. As if by learning one language he fears he might forget the other.

But he'll be fine, she tells herself, squeezing his hand, thinking how much she's looked forward to having him at her side. Not waiting, per se, but eager to show him her work, to share the pride she feels in helping women get loans from the bank, in keeping their morale up, in teaching them to care better for themselves and their children. The whole experience has made her think about the luxuries people take for granted. An effect she's anticipated, but not as much as it's hit her. How much she wants now to pare down her life, to live and love with an honesty even more committed and conscious than she knew in college. True, she's going to this resort, she tells herself, pushing away a twinge of guilt. But sun and water—that's pretty elemental. And who doesn't need a little indulgence once in a while? She wants Anthony to realize how hard she works, and how hard the work is, even if he didn't seem to understand yesterday. She tries not to worry about the question he asked. Is that all she does—teach women how to wash their eggs and stack their breads? But he listened carefully when she detailed her other jobs, when she told him how the women's voices often echo in her head. *She's too sick to work. Her husband beats her. He doesn't let her sell her own things.*

So what if in the end he made a joke of it all. "And do you teach the egg ladies not to count their eggs before they hatch?" (Like they have time to joke!) But he was only teasing, she tells herself, remembering how he's loved her emails. The first ones about the women's blackened teeth, the cracks in their heels, the knots of muscle on the backs of their legs. And soon after that, the ones about their faces as they concentrate on counting their money, every last *peso*, the ones about their persistence, their pride. "Send pictures," he requested. "Too intrusive," she answered. But she kept writing. *The women nurse their babies in the open, here. They wear beautiful colors, here. Full skirts in blue or red. They braid their hair in two tight braids and have wide brown faces. Round and beautiful.*

"Like yours," he emailed back with a smiley face, telling her he couldn't wait for August, to hold her in his arms, to share this place she's come to love.

"But look," he says as they wait on the bench. He points to the cages at the far end of the soccer field adjoining the factory. Does she think anyone would mind if they go take a look? The soccer field has a high wire fence around it. They'll need to push open the gate. But they've paid for the resort, haven't they? And this is all part of the resort, isn't it?

In a way, Carrie loves how Anthony almost runs across the barren field, unable to take his eyes off the three black spider monkeys in the first cage who begin to pace then run in circles as he approaches. Round and round the monkeys go, hitting the wire mesh sides with such force, the whole cage bulges and clangs. He can't believe how close they can get, he says, staring as the monkeys slam onto the front and hang in perfect stillness. One plasters himself upright, his dark lips peeled back over his pink gums, hissing. The other two brace sideways, their furry arms and legs extended so far, so effortlessly, Anthony says he has to laugh. Under their gaze, he feels, well, a little sheepish, he says, smiling. "And utterly useless." He lifts his arms as if to show his inadequacy, gazing as the monkeys resume their circuit—looping from side to side, bar to rope, never missing a grip as they skim by each other in hair-raising static, then freeze once more and stare. "They must find us strange!" he says, stepping yet closer to the cage.

"But they're monkeys," Carrie says, surprised at the cautionary tone in her voice. He seems almost too caught up in the monkeys.

"Likely they don't find us anything, right?" she says, trying to sound casual with this little reality check.

"Oh?" he says with a grin. "And how can you be so sure?" He bends over, starts to swing his arms and lope, but goes only a few strides before he stands up, blushes a little, and laughs. She has to laugh too.

"You don't ever change, do you?" she says, hoping to sound reassuring.

"Nope," he quips, grinning as he reaches out for her hand.

But first he needs to clean his glasses. "Dust," he says, this clipped word rolling out of his mouth as easily as all the others she's been teaching him.

"But it's not *polvo*," she blurts out so fast he looks at her with alarm. "They don't say 'dust blows into our houses here.' Or even 'dirt,'" she insists, knowing the urgency in her voice could be confused for admonition. But she's only trying to express her love of this language, this place! "Not *tierra*, but *la tierra*!" she says, raising her arms in a big circle over her head. "'The EARTH blows into our houses.' I love it," she exclaims, bringing her arms down like a platter, as if she could hand him the whole planet right now.

He opens his arms in readiness. But the monkeys start bashing again. She drops her hands. Steps back.

"Look," he says, clearly hoping to regain her attention. Beyond the cage, four large peacocks cross back and forth, dragging their tails. "Look at the dust," he says. "I mean the EARTH," he corrects himself, gazing at their tails. He's studying to be an engineer, to build bridges one of these days. Carrie can feel him puzzling. How the heck do they raise those tails? "Check out their necks," he calls out. "Shimmering blue! And their headdresses," he adds, putting his fingers straight up on his head to imitate.

"You mean their crests," she calls out before she can stop herself. (But that's what they're called!)

"Sure, crests. Dust. The EARTH. Whatever," he says as he walks toward the birds, thrusting his head, doing the Egyptian, waiting for her to laugh again. Which she does, partly because she's always loved his antics, and partly because she's grateful he doesn't seem fazed by her insistence.

By the time the little white Toyota taxi finally arrives with three Bolivians already in it, Carrie is more than ready to head for the resort. After an hour of watching animals, she's ready to plunge into a pool and hide away—from herself, of all things, she realizes, surprised by the impatience welling up in her. Maybe it's good they're going to this resort, after all. Maybe she needs an escape from work more than she realizes. A pool, yes, but also some torchlight, crowds, dancing to help her forget herself a little. This will be fun, she says to herself, smiling with relief and even amusement when the driver directs Anthony to the makeshift jump seat lodged over the handbrake between the front seats.

(No way her butt is going to fit in that spot!) She's glad Anthony will get the sudden immersion he wants. He'll be fine, she tells herself as he cranes his neck around to look at her in the backseat between two men with market sacks filled with vegetables. He raises his eyebrows in gleeful anticipation, even though she knows he won't like being perched up there—and without a seatbelt. She hasn't told him, nobody here wears seatbelts.

But he'll deal, she tells herself for the last time as they bump down the driveway, Anthony clutching the seats, being careful, she can tell, not to touch the driver, the gear shift, the ceramic Jesus swinging from the mirror, or the young woman next to him dressed in a white blouse and fitted black skirt. Carrie settles back to enjoy the adventure, trying not to worry about this unexpected feeling of responsibility that tugs at her. This need to make sure he not only likes Bolivia, but understands it. And not just understands, but something deeper, though she's not sure whether that means loving Bolivia or just welcoming it. Including the smell of pig fat, which fills the car just now, as if seeping from everyone's skin. Except theirs, of course. Or maybe, it dawns on her for the first time, except Anthony's. Has he already smelled pig fat on her and said nothing?

She's relieved when the men on either side of her seem to settle in, as if they feel her ease at being in this little car. Until she notices them staring at the resort brochure she's embarrassed to be clutching in her hand. "Yes, we're going for a little dip," she says in her fluent Spanish, trying to sound apologetic as she folds the brochure and tucks it into her backpack. She wishes she were holding one of her business cards instead. *Pro Mujer*. See what she's doing "for women" in their country? She's glad the driver starts up a conversation. "*¿Cómo se llama?*" She'll be able to explain herself.

But he's not asking her. He's asking Anthony.

There's a long pause. As she waits, she realizes her legs have become stuck to the vinyl in this heat. Brazen her, wearing shorts for a change instead of the pants and long skirts she usually wears in deference to the people she works with. But she does nothing to unstick herself yet, not wanting to disrupt what she knows is Anthony's concentration, his desire to respond to this simple question by himself. They've practiced it often, but this time she knows he doesn't want to hear her voice in the mix—and nor, she's surprised to realize, does she. How odd this worry of hers, not a worry she's felt before, that the men will laugh at him when they see he's at her mercy, a woman as his guide. Or is it her they'll be laughing at? She pulls her lips closed, an invitation it seems for the women's voices again to fill her mind. *I cannot get out today. My children are sick today. My husband says my working is making them sick.* Just try your best, she tells them. Be strong, like me, and speak up, she's wanted to say, thinking of the man on the street corner in Tarija who rushed at her one day with his Mormon Bible. How quickly she turned on him. Why was he obeying *los*

70

hombres blancos? She wasn't one of them. Not here to convert or be converted. Leave her alone.

But now in the car she says nothing. For Anthony's sake, she tells herself. Not wanting to embarrass him. She's grateful when the driver speaks up. "*Me llamo Enrique.*"

"*Me llamo Antoine,*" Anthony's voice rings out almost immediately, just the cue he needed, though why he adds the French flourish is beyond her. Maybe it's pride or maybe relief. Or maybe, she realizes as she sees his fingers gripping the seats, it's their overloaded taxi, and the two trucks poking along ahead of them, and the way Enrique keeps going out and back to check for an opening in the oncoming traffic that makes Anthony embellish. As they weave in and out, she can almost feel his urge to call out from his perch, "Not yet. Don't pass." Or maybe just "No"—that useful little word in almost any language.

But as Enrique swerves into the other lane, Anthony keeps his mouth shut. Carrie has to admit, even as her heart races, she's glad he says nothing. Things are different here. You need to go with the flow, she thinks, remembering her own fear when she first arrived and rode in the trucks out to the *campo*, bouncing through rocky gullies, bursting with speed, the women sitting in the back with her grinning as she grabbed for whatever she could get hold of. But she's made it just fine, she tells herself, letting out her breath as Enrique gets back into their lane. They *will* get to the resort, preferably alive, she jokes to herself—smiling to think this is something Anthony would say. Yes, they'll swim *and* dance, she decides with greater conviction. One *can* step out of one world and into another. Easily, she assures herself, buoyed by the breathtaking vistas out her window—sweeping fields of grass, tall skinny trees with leaves expanding endlessly at the very top, billows of clouds rising in the distance. Must be where the jungle begins. Moisture in the air. Heat rising. Something like that. She's never been to the jungle before.

A first for both of them, she muses as she studies the sweat lines on Anthony's neck, thinking how new but old it felt last night to run her hands along his body, marking every boundary and curve. She'll take him to Tarija afterwards and show him the real Bolivia, she promises herself, feeling better now as she anticipates their stroll into town for dinner, their dancing the night away. Maybe they'll even put on their bathing suits and sit on those silly bar stools in the water, sip their drinks, and listen to the jungle animals croon in the distance. They'll be fine, she tells herself as the car slows down for the first of many white-striped speed bumps that mark the little towns, where young boys wave water bottles near the car windows, as if *gringos* were thirstier than most, or just not smart enough to carry their own water, as she and Anthony are carrying theirs.

Miles later when Enrique turns off the highway, even though she resists her temptation to perch forward to look for signs of the resort, the men on either side of her chuckle, as if they can feel her anticipation. Inwardly, she again fights off her embarrassment. She knows how incongruous the resort will be in this little town of narrow streets, adobe houses, terracotta roofs, and verandas lined with the red flowers she loves. But she's not going to let them put a damper on her little detour. She keeps looking for the large vases filled with sumptuous flowers that will surely mark the entrance, for the long driveway edged with white-painted stones. For a moment she even wonders if the men beside her conjure up similar pictures, unwilling to admit they might be envious, even as they try to appear full of amusement.

"*¿Paraíso Eco Resort, aquí?*" Anthony's question pierces the quiet, surprising her as perhaps it surprises everyone. He sounds like a native.

"*No, no, estoy dejando aquí otra pasajera. Mi hija va a la corte para una cita,*" Enrique replies, as if he and Anthony have been conversing for hours.

When Anthony nods as if he's understood the whole reply, Carrie smiles. Of course it's only "no" he's responding to—which is really all the information he needs. But she leans forward anyway—so what if she speaks English at this point—to translate for him. Enrique's daughter, the young woman beside him, has a meeting at the courthouse. "She must be in trouble," Carrie adds, seeing the thick black folder the young woman takes from her feet, the way she clutches it in her lap, the way her long black hair sweeps over her face as if she wants it there. Carrie's surprised when Enrique turns around and glares at her. Is something wrong?

Or is it this scene unfolding before them that puts Enrique on edge? How many times, with *gringos* in his car, has he pulled up to these stone steps, to this group of young men talking and smoking, who begin their catcalls even before his daughter opens the door. *Ey linda, ven aquí. Te quiero, mi amor.* How much they love her, want her, need a wife! Come here, girl! Their voices grate and screech.

Carrie feels her own body tense. What woman wouldn't tense? But there's more here than just their taunts pulling at her, she realizes. She sits very still, her lips pressed together, not liking this weight that again seems to be holding her back. Not her knowledge she can't order Enrique to get out, accompany his daughter up the stairs, and tell the young men to shut up. Not even the glare she gets from Anthony—because he doesn't turn around, doesn't say a thing. But just his presence makes her feel suddenly careful. Suddenly wary of upsetting a delicate balance. She feels her chest grow tight. She wants to speak up for Enrique's daughter, for the women she works for, for the roar of voices in her head.

But she says nothing as Enrique's daughter heads up the stairs, holding her purse and folder tight against her side, ignoring the men as they snicker, flash their eyebrows, and reach out as if to skim her legs, until Carrie can't stand it anymore. Her heart racing, her words rushing through her mind, she hears herself whisper not, *No les hagas caso. Encuentra tu propio camino*, the first words that fill her head, but "Don't let them bother you. Find your own path." She needs at least Anthony to hear her speak, to know she's the same Carrie as always.

The cords in his neck tighten as he turns around, puts his finger to his lips to shush her, then turns quickly back, just as Enrique, who also whips his head around, points to the empty seat and says in slow but perfect English, "You, Antoine, you sit here now."

Carrie is still trembling three miles later, when Enrique, having gotten back onto the highway, puts on his signal and pulls far enough into a short dirt driveway so the RED MEAT truck barreling behind them makes the little car shimmy, but doesn't pull it back onto the road. She can't stop thinking about Anthony's warning. Be careful how you meddle. Be careful about being too strong. How odd to feel judged by him.

And yet you love him, she hears herself saying, hating how she feels caught between her love for herself and her love for him, feeling her confusion so intensely she almost misses Enrique's announcement, "*Paraíso Eco Resort.*" She's not sure whether it's the mock flourish in his voice or something else that makes the men beside her chuckle. She looks up to follow their eyes. Immediately in front of them is not a long driveway edged with stones but a white fence with tall, spear-like balusters that stretch across the property. In the middle of the fence, in a little glass guard-house, sits a Bolivian man in a white shirt, black pants, and gold-rimmed captain's hat. Poised on his stool, he stares at them as if he's been waiting all day. Beyond him, a single-level concrete hotel extends along a palm-lined patio (at least there're palms), which meanders around a huge serpentine pool. There in the middle of the pool, under a thatched roof, is the piano bar, connected to the patio by the kind of arched bridge one sees in a Japanese garden.

If Anthony is disappointed, or feeling her confusion, he doesn't let on. He says nothing as they walk past the pool that glistens in the sunlight, past the empty patio chairs and tables, past the hammocks hung without a quiver, past the long row of hotel rooms to the manager's office at the far end. As they pass, not a door opens or closes. Not a soul wanders down the mosaic paths. He also voices no disappointment when they open their bedroom door to find a flimsy double bed, a casement window too high to look out of, a little bathroom with a plastic shower stall, and a TV with a placard boasting 64 channels. Carrie hears only her internal sigh as she stands in the middle of the room, realizing how much she really did want something fancy—not a confession she plans to share with Anthony on this trip.

But at least the pool is here, she tells herself. And it appears they'll have it all to themselves, she announces, pretending this ghost resort doesn't bother her a bit. Once she gets her sun, her swim, everything will be fine, she tells herself, seeing him eye the bed, knowing he's contemplating a siesta of sorts, but knowing she needs to go swimming first. Does he mind?

"*No hay problema*," he says with extra vehemence, as if maybe he feels her disappointment after all.

Next to the pool, the sun beating down on her as she lies on a plastic lounge chair, Carrie quiets herself, thinking how good it feels to fulfill this simple wish—to get good and hot before anything else. She closes her eyes, trying not to hear the trucks rumbling by. Or to smell their exhaust. Or to feel the grime rising and settling on every table and ledge, in every tuck of flesh. The EARTH finding its way, she tells herself with a sigh, maybe relieved the place isn't so fancy after all. Without the crowds and the hoopla, maybe they'll be able to talk more about how she loves Bolivia, loves her job, even contemplates staying longer. They'll have time to talk about that odd moment in the taxi, too, how he shushed her. Did he mean to do that? Maybe she needs to come right out and tell him how odd it feels to have him here. Of course she loves it. Loves him. Loves his silly ways. They make her laugh. But he needs to support her desire to speak up, she almost calls out as she feels the water he's flicking on her legs, which feels good in this heat. She opens her eyes and squints into the sunlight at him. Droplets of water glisten on his sweeping blond hair.

"You coming in?" he asks. He puckers his lips as if to kiss her, pats the water and then the raft he holds alongside. "It's wonderful," he says with exaggeration.

"So you were worried, too?" she chances, hearing what sounds like his uncertainty.

"Worried?" He flicks water at her again. "Why worry when we can dance tonight under the stars. If there's room on the dance floor, that is."

She shakes her head, chuckling, trying to let go of her worries, grateful in a way for his insistence. "You're such a dreamer, aren't you?" she says, wanting her words to sound like a compliment.

For a moment he holds still, furrowing his brow. "Hey," he says finally. He pats the water again. "*Agua. Agua*. Why don't you come in and play?"

For a while, as they float around the pool, their arms lightly splayed across their backs so as to hold their rafts together, they say nothing. Carrie likes how the current guides them around the circumference, past the empty lounge chairs, under the bridge that arcs to the piano bar, along the gardens where tropical flowers create their own colorful mosaic. She closes her eyes, enjoying how she can almost forget where she is. Can feel their bodies relaxing in the water, as if maybe the actual place where they're together doesn't finally matter. It's love that counts, she thinks, still trying to put her worries behind her. Maybe she'll just tell him it feels odd to have someone—anyone!—at her side. She reaches out to pull his raft closer.

Love Boundaries

"Hey," he says, as if he's been waiting for exactly this invitation. He smiles, flicks water at her face. Can they talk about a few things now, things they both might have on their minds?

For a second she feels silly. All this time assuming he's just rolling along, not noticing the bumps, when in fact he's been collecting concerns, too. He wants to talk, just as she does. She breathes an easy sigh of relief, nodding as his face turns serious. What, he wants to know, does she teach her egg ladies once they've mastered the basics?

She pauses a moment. Why is he asking the same old thing? But maybe he needs time to warm up to the real stuff. Okay. One more time, she repeats herself. She advises them about—she relishes these words as they flow off her tongue—"*los anticonceptivos, atención médica prenatal, la violencia doméstica.*" But now can they talk about more important things? She's glad to see his eyes light up. In her own mind, she starts to sort what she wants him to know. First about the women's voices. How much they've come to matter to her. And then about working for women in a bigger way. How committed she is to such work. Which is why that little scene in the taxi bothered her, she wants to say, unable to let go of it, needing him to understand how it felt.

But already he's talking. Does she plan to stay on for the year to teach the ladies?

He must see the surprised look on her face, the real question lurking there, because he quickly resumes talking. Of course he

79

wants to know all about her life in Bolivia. And of course he wants to support everything she does. But they've been together four years now. Isn't it time to make some decisions?

It's odd how the same tightness she felt in the taxi comes over her now. "But what about the women?" she asks, suddenly fearful he's missing something. She watches his face grow puzzled.

"What women?"

"The women the men hoot at," she says, trying to start slowly, but feeling her voice grow more insistent. "The women I work for. The men who put them down. Like you did with me in the taxi. When you looked at me like I should be quiet!" The words leap out before she can hold them back.

"But Carrie—!" She watches his deep blue eyes narrow with alarm. "What does that have to do with us?" he says. "Those men weren't harassing you. They didn't even care you were in the car! They don't care about you anymore than"—he looks around as if for a prop—"anymore than the guys who heat this pool or weed these gardens. What does any of that have to do with you or us? I mean—" he gestures toward the gardens, "it's their job to make these beautiful. Just like your women. It's their job to sell those eggs, those breads. And it's their job, too, to tell the men to stop harassing them. It's not up to you or even about you—"

Fortunately he stops. Stops when he sees her tilt her head and stare at him, not exactly sure how the pool or the gardens have come into this picture, but very clear of three things she

80

needs to tell him. "Anthony," she says softly but firmly. "They don't *have* to make the gardens beautiful. They choose to. Nor are they *'my'* women. Nor do they heat the pool." She points to the sun. "Why heat it when you have something like that?"

"Well you never know in a place like this," he says, the sharpness in his voice seeming to startle him as much as it startles her. "And why do you have to be so testy anyway, when I've come all this distance to be with you? What's got your goat?"

"I don't have a goat!" The words come out of her mouth so fast, it's as if she's been waiting for months to tell him not about pools or gardens or even women in the *campo*, but about choice and language and maybe love. About the luxury of those things. "I don't have a goat, any more than I have 'eggs' to count before they hatch," she says, making little quote marks in the air as she slips off her raft and stands in the waist-deep water. "Any more than the women here have the luxury to worry about 'eggs'"—she makes little quote marks again. "They have to worry about real *eggs*. About whether their hens will lay *eggs*. About whether people will buy *eggs*. About whether they'll be able to feed their families on the money from *eggs*. *Eggs*," she says again, hitting that word each time and cupping her hands as if she were holding real ones. "They don't have the time or energy or money to worry about other things," she nearly shouts, tears coming to her eyes. "Which is maybe why I'm here!"

"Okay! I got it," Anthony says. "*Eggs*," he repeats,. cupping his hands so as to stress his comprehension. "But, c'mon, Carrie. Could you lighten up a little?"

For a moment she says nothing. She feels suddenly tired, knowing how her little explosion has come up out of nowhere, or so it seems to Anthony. What was she trying to say, really? That people make choices when they have the luxury to make them. That they play with language when they have the luxury to play. That they indulge in love when they have the luxury for that, too, though here she hesitates, knowing how treacherous this whole idea is. As if poor people don't have the time or energy for love or choice, or even wordplay, which isn't at all what she means, though the insinuation is there, she has to admit. Just like the assumption—or is it the truth?—that's she's freer than they are, not really an insider, never an insider, but an outsider from the very start. How then can she be truly part of this place she loves?

This weight of uncertainty is what she takes with her as she closes her eyes and dunks her head backwards in the water, knowing she owes Anthony an apology, not for wanting his support, but for blowing up. When she resurfaces, water streaming down her face, she tells him she's sorry. It's silly, but for weeks she's been thinking about floating in a pool, feeling the hot sun soak into the marrow of her bones. She just needs to be able to do that without any questions, she tells him, and without any fears, though she doesn't mention this. Can he understand her need for a break? Before she gives him a chance to answer, she points to a bright red bird that's landed on the edge of the piano bar.

"*Tojo rojo, tojo rojo,*" she says, hoping he'll repeat the words after her, hoping he'll see how teaching a language can be a way of saying I'm sorry. Or I love you. Or maybe both.

For the rest of the afternoon, as they swim and lie on the hammocks reading, Carrie figures the worst is behind them. Until they go inside and discover the stark white flesh under their bathing suits, the crackling parchment of their sunburned skin. Until she cries out she should have known better, should have slathered on lotion to guard against the tropical sun, should have insisted they stay inside and take a siesta like everyone else. What a stupid *gringa* she's been! She knows she ought to be grateful when Anthony puts on her aloe and jokes about getting roasted, when he struts like a bird around the room calling "*rojo tojo, rojo tojo,*" not realizing he has the name backwards, when he insists on adding levity to life. But as she sits on the bed, she realizes there's no hiding from her own stupid mistakes or desires or even illusions. "Why did we come to this place?" she cries out. "Where is everyone? Look at this room. It's not the least bit fancy. And just look at us," she says, opening her arms and staring down at her bright red body. "We're as red as—

"Don't say anything," she says, looking up quickly, knowing he's dying to fill in the blank. As red as a tomato, a beet, a devil, a fire, a bleeding heart. But right now, she needs to fill in that blank herself. "As red as RED!" she calls out, pretending she doesn't see the grin breaking on his face or feel her own relief at the strength of her voice.

Later as they sit under torchlight on the terrace, drinking wine and watching the piano bar shimmer in neon light, if she seems a little distant to Anthony, he appears not to notice. It's not as if anything has changed, she tells herself, but only that she's trying to figure out how you balance between loving a person and the good ways he makes you feel and knowing your own life might be heading in a different direction. But a direction you want to share, even if it's different! she tells herself, grateful they'll be flying back to Tarija tomorrow. They won't be able to go to the jungle after all, she tells Anthony, because the real jungle is a half-day's drive away. If they were staying longer, the resort manager would happily take them up there and camp with them overnight, but obviously that's not in the picture. But the manager did say there are a few animals out back in cages, if they want to see them, Carrie adds, imagining Anthony won't be interested.

But he is, he says, his face lighting up. Of course they'll go see the animals. After they dance, that is.

Carrie waits to see him crack a smile. As if there's going to be dancing. Ha ha. Funny joke. She *does* love how he takes her to this edge of silliness, a distraction from herself. But he keeps sipping his wine so seriously, she can't stop herself from asking—Does he really believe there's going to be music tonight? She turns to look at the piano bar. Microphones unplugged in the corner. A grand piano in the middle, covered by a heavy drape.

"But, of course," he says so confidently Carrie wonders for a moment if maybe he's conversed with the manager on his own. "There'll be music tonight," he says again with gusto. "Even if I have to play it myself."

Carrie has to smile. "But you don't play piano, Anthony," she says very softly, an odd sadness coming over her, which she tries to push away.

"Oh? And how do you know?"

Carrie chuckles a little nervously. It's possible he's been taking lessons in her absence, but somehow she knows he's as far from playing the piano as he is from swinging in trees.

And yet that doesn't stop him. Without another word, he stands up, skirts the edge of the pool, crosses the bridge to the piano bar, takes a microphone, uncovers the piano, and sits down on the bench, first pulling out the tails of his tuxedo. As if he were wearing a tuxedo. Carrie feels that old touch of giddiness come over her as she watches him open the lid and take a deep breath, set his hands on the keys, stretch out his arms, and get ready to sway with the music. For a moment, again she doubts herself. Maybe he *has* been taking lessons, *has* been preparing this surprise for her, and the men behind her. She turns to see the wait-staff gathered on the edge of the patio. Maybe they've come to order him off the stage. To save her from what she wishes she feared more than anything else. That he'll turn on the microphone and belt out one of the few songs he actually knows.

"Anthony—?" Her voice rings out over the water as he gets up, unwinds the microphone cord, goes over to a socket, plugs it in, clears his throat, and gets ready to sing. She looks over her shoulder at the five Bolivian men standing in a line, smiling.

"Yes, Madam?" he calls out into the darkness. "Would you like to dance?"

Carrie sits still.

"Madam?" He calls out again. "Will you join me or must I escort you?"

She looks down into her lap. She knows he'll stand out there and call to her until she agrees. One little dance. Or until she says no. Flat out no. No translation needed.

"Or perhaps you'd like me to swim across?" he calls out, leaning over to untie his shoes. He takes them off. Peels off his socks. Stands up to unbutton his shirt. He must see the men grinning. Do they understand what he's saying, what he's doing, and what she's about to do, too?

Carrie stands up much sooner than she thought she would. She follows Anthony's path over the bridge to where they dance, at first in small circles near the piano as he hums one of their favorite old songs—"Fly me to the moon and let me play among the stars"—and then in bigger circles as he spins then sweeps her along the edge, dipping her so far her loose hair almost touches the water. As he arcs her back, she clutches onto his shoulders.

"Anthony, don't you dare," she says, trying not to think about what she knows she needs to tell him in the morning—how their lives will go on, how they can still love each other for a long time, how visiting Tarija will still be fun. "Ridiculous is one thing, water quite another," she whispers fiercely into his ear.

"So true," he says, but not until they both come up sputtering, both of them surprised, both of them with their clothes plastered to their bodies, their wet hair streaming down their faces.

"Oh, Anthony," she says, finding her feet and looking down at her summer dress flattened and transparent against her body. She ducks down as if she can hide. "Now what?"

"Now we swim across and get out," he says like a tour director who's done this countless times. He takes her hand and laughs as he half-swims, half-walks, marveling at how his pant legs feel like fins, at how this last splash was sure a great one, at how they'll remember this for a long time.

Carrie figures they're in for the night, but Anthony will have none of that. "We need to see the animals," he says. He wants to know what they're like at night. Restless or asleep? But also, he admits, he wants to walk with her. To guide her down the paths, to be as close to the jungle as they might ever get in the future. "If there is a future," he adds at the last second, a flash of worry in his eyes.

"Now what do we have here?" he asks as they approach the

first cage, ablaze with a spotlight from the back of the hotel. Carrie stands quietly next to him as they study the guinea fowl with an elaborate crest. "Ah," he says. "A bird with a pin cushion." He pauses, tilting his head as if waiting to hear a voice from the jungle. "Oh, no. I mean a crest," he says. He squeezes her hand.

So kind and funny, Carrie says to herself, wondering what he's thinking.

At the next cage, two little squirrel monkeys cling to the front, their tiny butterscotch limbs tucked close to their bodies, their flesh-colored fingers and long toes curled over the wire. Anthony kneels down—to get eye-level, he says, so as not to scare them. Aloud he muses—is it fear or longing in their eyes? Or something else? He pauses before he points toward the wrinkled bottoms of their feet that press against the fence. "Like the imprint of newborns," he says as if talking to himself, until he turns, stands up, and asks her directly. "But what do *you* think?" Somehow she knows he's not waiting for her to say their feet look soft, as if you could touch them.

"I think it's hard to be alone," she says quietly, surprised these words find their way out.

He nods, reaching out to take her hand as he goes to read the official label on the cage. "*Saimiri-sciureu-ardilla-squir-rel-mon-key*," he says, enunciating each syllable as if he were learning—or maybe teaching—another language.

Go Fish

Wait—is that a quiver? Marcie reels in a little. Waits. Reels in a little more. Holds still. Is there something there? She gives a jerk. Just a little jerk. Might this be her chance? As she stands on a rock beside a string of small mountain lakes high in the Wind Rivers of Wyoming, she thinks about the words she said playfully to Daniel the other night, as if joking were the only way she could admit her desire. *Teach me how to kill and I'll tell you how I like it.* Even as she says the words to herself now, she draws in a quick breath. Imagine wanting to kill something. Imagine knowing what that feels like and discovering you like the feeling. Surely it must release something. But what?

For a moment she pauses to gaze at Daniel over in the next lake, planted so firmly up to his thighs she can feel the pull between him and the invisible fish. Back and forth, back and forth, he casts his line in a mesmerizing sweep of cursive. In between casts, he holds perfectly still, waiting—as he puts it—for the fly to set, the shadow to rise, the pocket to rip open, for the suck of water that begins it all. Then comes the part he likes best, he tells her. The part he dreams about. Not the steel-rimmed mouth clamping down on his fly, but the ensuing dance, the rush of his line in and out, in and out, whirring as he lets the fish dive, then taut as he reels it in, tightness gathering in his lower arm and shoulder as he slowly brings the fish to shore. If this is living, he says, he'll take it.

And so will she, she tells herself, trying not to worry or wonder—suppose she doesn't catch a fish? Suppose after all this energy she's put into thinking about catching a fish, killing something, she can't finally pull it off? She takes a deep breath. She's felt so proud of her determination to bring about this moment on the cusp of thirty and maybe even marriage, when she knows it's time to put aside once and for all a suspicion that keeps haunting her—if she's hiding one deep urge, what else might she be hiding, hiding in a way that makes her ultimately dishonest, hiding in a way Daniel is not?

Or so it appears he's not, she tells herself, wrapping her hand tighter around the cork handle, determined to believe his ease with fishing is just that. Ease with a sport. A fun sport. An innocent sport, he's told her. *Try it for yourself and you'll see.*

Yes, try it, she tells herself, knowing there's no good reason to doubt his kindness, his gentleness, no reason to fear his fishing might speak to how he'll treat her. How some people laugh at her. Oh, there you go again, Marcie—always worrying about women.

90

Go Fish

Don't you ever give it up?

Yes, in fact, I do. I can. I will, she tells herself, bracing her feet on the rock as she prepares to feel that sudden little tug. But also deciding in that moment not to be one with that untethered slippery beast circling her hook, no doubt, but to be one with her rod. To think of herself as a water witch, alert to vibrations. Yes, vibrations, she says, feeling the hum on her lips as she closes her eyes a little tighter and presses her hand onto the cork, waiting, reeling in *just a little*, jerking *just a little*, reeling in some more, getting ready to feel that special feeling, a bite, a fish, almost a fish! But then pausing. Not liking what she feels. The lightness of her line. She opens her eyes. Her bobber floats near the water's edge. Her hook rests on the leaves in the shallows. All her fish eggs gone, again.

"Goddamnit," she whispers, cranking in the line, not caring if the bobber pulls tight against the tip, half wishing it would all break. "I give up!" she yells as if to herself, but really to him. His idea to come fishing. His intoning the beauty of this place.

It doesn't take Daniel long to wade out of the lake, prop his pole on some beach rocks, and clamber over. She knows from four years of living with him, ever since they graduated from Wharton, that he'll sit next to her and peer into her face from under his thick eyebrows. "Having a hard time?" he'll ask. "Want me to cast for you?" But he says nothing when he sits down, staring instead over the smooth water just beginning to darken, the sun sinking toward the mountain peaks. Out of the corner of her eye, she studies his profile. The sharp corner of his cheekbone. The ridge of his deep-set eyes.

"You know," he says finally, "you don't have to catch a fish." He squints toward the sky as if the sun were still high and bright.

Marcie takes a big breath and shakes her head. But she wants to catch a fish! she tells him. They've come all this way from DC. She's made up her mind, is ready to catch a fish. But she can't even keep her stupid little salmon eggs on the hook, she cries, bemoaning how the fish nibble at them. Maybe she should just admit it, she says, hoping he'll beg otherwise. Fishing might not be her thing.

She's only half relieved when he grins. She knows what he's thinking—how last summer she surprised everyone, most of all herself, by catching a small perch with a drop line off the Wellfleet town pier. Twenty feet down to the water. Not expecting to catch anything or to heed his words. *Give it a jerk*. Which she did. A regular heave-ho so huge the fish shot out of the water, soared above their heads in a big circle, and landed smack on the other side of the crowded wharf on the blanket of an old couple sitting in the sun eating bologna sandwiches. How the couple laughed when the fish landed. Clapped their hands. *What a hitter. Sign her up for the big leagues.*

"But did I kill it?" Marcie wanted to know, not ready to kill anything then.

"It'll be okay," Daniel said, showing her how to twist it gently off the hook. The prongs on its fin cut her hand. The salt stung. She'd be okay, he insisted, telling her to throw the fish back, reassuring her when it hit the water and floated. *Only stunned. It'll be fine in a moment. Watch.*

Yes, watch, she tells herself, thinking about the eventual flick of the perch's tail as she follows Daniel's gaze across the lake and up. The dying of the day, she thinks, when the colors of the sun start to pour down the mountainsides and flow into the lake, as if all color begins up here. If you weren't here now, you wouldn't see this beauty, she tells herself, thinking how she loves the remoteness, the enormous spread of quiet, the chance to be here with Daniel. She feels a quiver run through her body. A quiver like the one she felt that day in Wellfleet. Was it from catching a fish or watching it go free?

"I know you'll be a great fisherwoman," he whispers as he leans close and puts his arm around her. "In the meanwhile, be a great fish," he teases, playing his lips along her cheek, suctioning in the chubby part. *If you were a fish, you'd have a tender morsel right here.* She smiles as he pretends to chomp down, knowing how earnest and pleased he is at her willingness to give this sport a try. "Keep trying," he whispers. "Just one." Then he repeats the magic words. *Flick. Thumb. Arc. Line. Stopper. Fish.*

Yes, fish, she says to herself, watching him bound back to his lake. She takes three more eggs, presses them onto her hook, stands up on her rock, and prepares to throw the whole works forward. *Just concentrate on the flick and everything else will follow.*

But as hard as she tries, she can't seem to bring in a fish. She gets better at casting, a lovely arc in the air, but as she reels in yet another empty hook, she feels her whole body tighten. How silly to be upset over a fish! Like she's a failure in life just because she can't catch a goddamn fish.

But she wants to catch a fish! she nearly calls out, not liking how she's starting to wonder if there's something in the universe trying to tell her she's not meant to fish. Or is something deep in her heart holding her back? (Why her heart and not his?) She turns to watch Daniel casting, to listen to the sweep of his line, the scything of the air unexpectedly soothing to her. As soothing as the quiet of the aspens and the echo of emptiness in this huge mountain sky. He loves these things, too, she says to herself. None of it changes if you catch a fish.

As if she's ever going to catch a fish, she says to herself with every failed attempt, wishing she didn't feel more and more like an impostor, didn't feel herself tense when Daniel comes over to see if he can help, to tell her she doesn't need to catch a fish, didn't feel this profound regret coming over her. Whatever she's hiding inside, it's never going to come out.

"You make it sound so easy," she says, her edge of impatience clear when Daniel tells her not to worry about fishing. Just take in the beauty of this place. He gestures toward the lake, the trees, the mountains, the open sky. She stares into the shallow water where pine needles crisscross the sodden leaves, where the lake glosses over, nothing disturbing its surface. If only he'd admit it's *not* easy.

"But it *is* easy," he says, chuckling at her frustration. "Once you get the hang of it, that is." He peers at her from under his thick eyebrows as he flicks his wrist a few times, pretends to hear his line whistle through the air, to see it soar, to feel it splash when it lands. He grins.

She pauses a second, staring at his hand, his flicks, as if he thinks she's talking about casting. "That's not what I mean," she says. Her reply comes out sharper than she intends.

"Then what *do* you mean, Marcie?" he asks, his reply sharper too.

Again she pauses. How quickly their conversation has changed. She gestures toward the lake as if it can help her. How can he catch fish and still be at one with this beauty? she asks. She waits while he stares out over the lake until finally he speaks, his voice low in his throat. Has she forgotten? They've had this conversation already. Fishing is just a sport. Fun. People do it all the time. She'll get the hang of it. Now, does she want him to cast for her? He puts his hand under her chin, holds her gently, peering into her eyes.

If only she could say yes. But doesn't he worry *at all* about killing fish? she has to ask first.

His face softens. He leans closer and smiles. "Marcie," he says, his lips close to hers. She waits to hear his reassurance, his words of understanding. Of course she's worried, he'll say. And of course he loves her for her worry, her depth, her honesty. But killing a fish doesn't change you or taint you, she gets ready to hear, to be reminded, once and for all, she tells herself as he pulls her closer, that it's okay to fish. She feels herself soften as he whispers, his breath warm on her ear. "Marcie," he pauses, "has anyone ever told you you think too much?"

He must feel her body stiffen.

"But it's true," he says, his whispering more intense. "Thinking keeps you from having fun, from enjoying simple pleasures. You know what I mean?"

She stands very still.

"I'm just telling the truth," he says, reaching out to take her hand. "Didn't we promise to tell the truth?"

She manages to nod, even as she wants to cry out—How can she stop thinking when she's a thinker, when she loves her thinking, when it's so much a part of who she is, when they were talking about fishing. Not her, but him! About his killing fish!

"Hey, listen," he says, talking a little faster. He points at the water, at the circles. The fish are there, he says. He'll put on a new hook. A bigger one. A winner! Wouldn't she like that?

Before she can object, he takes out his knife, cuts her old line, threads a new hook, ties it fast, and squeezes on two lead sinker balls with his teeth. He holds the rod out to her, his eyes eager and hopeful, but she shakes her head. "You don't get it, do you?" she says. "I'm not talking about fish. I'm talking about life!"

"But I love you, and you know it," he says pushing the rod toward her.

She shakes her head again. "No, you love *fishing*!" she says, though she knows he loves her too.

For a second, his nostrils flare. "And what's wrong with loving fishing?" he asks with a new edge of defiance.

She pauses, knowing she's repeating herself, knowing this circling over the same stuff can be as dangerous as the stuff itself. "If you love this place so much, why do you catch fish?"

Daniel tilts his head and stares at her. "We need to eat supper, Marcie," he says full of gravity. "And otherwise, as you know, I catch and release."

Again she pauses, surprised by the honesty welling up in her. "But why even catch and release?" she asks softly. "Why not just leave the fish alone?"

For a few moments he says nothing. Then he turns to her, his brow creased, worry in his eyes. "You think I'm a killer, Marcie?" he asks. He speaks with such restraint, it's as if he's holding his breath. "You think I'm going to hurt you?"

The way he puts it, the answer seems so obvious. She shakes her head.

"Marcie, it's just a sport," he says, almost pleading it seems. "You want to try again?" He holds out the rod for her.

"No thanks," she says quietly. "You do it. I'll watch."

Of course it takes Daniel only a few casts before he brings in a fat glistening rainbow trout. Marcie is feeling better. Their exchange, however painful, has cleared the air enough so she can joke with him again. That fish is hers, she says, meaning to be playful, assuring. They can still be one, can't they?

"Oh?" he asks. His eyes light up with the challenge. "Shall we see?" Before she has a chance to answer, he takes the trout by the tail and whacks its head hard against the rock. He must see her flinch. "We need to eat, Marcie, remember?" he says, a hint of warning in his voice.

She nods. But the blow came so quickly. As quickly as Daniel kneels down and slices the fish open along the bottom, like cutting a sewing pattern on a dotted line. Marcie has to admit she's curious. She peers over his shoulder, waiting to see the blood, surprised when there're only intestines and a bloated stomach, which he holds up in his palm. "Shall we?" But he's already pressing the point of his knife into the sac, slicing it to reveal not minnows or bugs or even babies, but four red gelatinous eggs. He looks up at Marcie, a grin on his face. "C'mon now. Laugh."

And she does. Not because he tells her to, but because this feat seems too amazing for words or design. Imagine. He's caught her fish.

"You know, we make a good team," he says. He bends over

to wash his hands in the water then stands up with a playful grunt. "You feed. Me hunt. Now, we cook."

"No, you cook," she says quickly, knowing he's been planning all along to prepare a feast for them. Fried trout. Steamed rice slathered in butter. Tomatoes he's hidden in his pack. She doesn't realize how hungry she is until they start eating, their mouths and fingers greasy with every bite, the fish succulent as it flakes apart, the fried tomatoes dripping down her lips, the rice as full and lingering in its buttery sweetness as the best of desserts hidden away in a secret spot. When they're done, Daniel says he'll do the dishes later. He wants to try his luck in his lake. Does she mind?

Maybe it's her full belly or the smell of fire in her hair or the crimson sunset filling her lake, or maybe it's the invitation not to think that makes her content to go sit on her rock, pick up her pole, and try casting again, just for the heck of it. What fish would be so stupid as to bite an empty hook? When her bobber lands out farther than before, she laughs. So be it, she thinks, or tries not to think. She doesn't jerk or reel in. She simply sits and gazes at the red plastic bobber. How odd to see how it keeps bobbing. But why, she wonders (wondering isn't thinking, is it?). No tide here. No wind. No waves. Could it be the sway of the earth? The pull of the unrisen moon? The magnetism of true north?

She turns to look toward Daniel, as if he could answer. He's still on the rocky beach, crouched over his tackle box. Let him do his own thing, she tells herself, feeling drawn toward him, toward what he's thinking right now, even if he wouldn't call it thinking. If he were a fish or a lake or a god, what would he bring forth tonight? Would it be a cranefly with its great wisps of pheasant tail and green fluorescent floss? Or a dark olive with its pointed starling wings and tail jutting back in a bristle of olive cock hackle? Or would it be a damsel nymph? "A proven killer," he loves to tease her, quoting from the book he reads at night, *Sex, Death, and Fly-Fishing*. But this is the fly he loves the most, he tells her, wanting her to come close. To touch the cobalt and orange lamb's wool wrapped around the hook. "So soft and unexpected," he says. "Look here at the tail feathers splayed like a spider mum. You love flowers, yes?"

Marcie takes a deep breath, determined to let go of her fear, her worry. To stop herself from remembering (is that thinking?) the feathers and pelts he's strewn across her dining room table, cutting them up as if they were never alive. As if to catch fish (and release!) were just part of life. She's determined to focus on this ease as she watches him walk into the water and begin casting back and forth in magical loops, writing on the sky. She closes her eyes, focusing on her love for him, panicking only for a moment when she opens her eyes to discover he's gone. Gone in a cloud of white, a haze so thick it's as if he were never there. In an instant, her heart racing, she knows what he'll say later to his friends, his voice full of passion. *Mayflies burst forth in the high mountains that night. I picked right. A caddis cast just where the shadow rose, where the pocket ripped open, where the mouth, agape, snapped and dashed into the depths.*

But will he catch the fish? She feels herself tense as he lets out the whirring line then reels it in, out and in, arched back then bent forward, as if paying homage to the lake, the fish, all the while backing slowly toward shore. His net is on the rocks, several feet from the water's edge. Will he get to it before the fish, in one dashing leap, catches slack and dives the other way? Will he call for her help? She reels in her line, sets her pole down, and stands up, waiting to hear him call for her, watching as he inches backward, not taking his eyes off the fish, the fish breaking the surface now, roiling the water, flicking its big fat tail. Marcie holds her breath. Yes, this will all work out, she lets herself think. The triumph of the catch. The triumph of the release.

Daniel looks quickly over his shoulder toward his net. But he's not moving back now. He's crouching forward as if to keep his body hidden from the fish. Just one more time he reels back, the pole bending to the point of breaking—surely it will snap. Surely the fish will go free. But, no. Drawing one hand back while keeping the other on the rod, he yanks the fish into the air, takes aim, and swats the glistening body hard and flat against the side of its head. In an instant stunned, the fish falls by Daniel's side. For a moment, he too stands motionless, stunned by his own success. Then he raises his face beaming toward Marcie.

This is not the ending she expects. To feel her heart racing, her legs trembling. To see his face light up in surprise. In joy. To feel how the innocence of the kill draws her in. How he draws her in. The way he sweeps his line back and forth. And puts eggs on her hook. And bites down on those lead balls, wincing as if it hurts. And now, the way he holds out the fish to her, in both hands, an offering. Come see our prize.

She threads the rocks to join him. He's washing his hands in the water. He's telling her how lucky he's been and grinning. He saying they'll have to eat the fish now. No way to keep it cold until morning. Is she hungry?

Is she what? Suddenly she stops. She stares at the big beautiful fish in his arms. A shimmering rainbow trout. "But we had dinner," she says, wondering if he hears the tremor in her voice, waiting for him to throw the fish back, thinking, at any moment now he'll do that.

Don't Let the Bastards Grind You Down

First he gives her a T-shirt. Red with bucking broncos and a large gold horseshoe tilted up. "For good luck," he says. Then a bottle of scotch. Glenlivet. Her favorite. "It's not a matter of finding someone who's available," he says, slinging his heavy arm over her shoulders. "It's a matter of becoming available."

Darcy kneads her empty ring finger. She can't get over the indentation in the bone.

"Come for a drink with the guys?" he asks after dinner, his hand cupped over her shoulder. They've just arrived in Syracuse at a summer conference for physical therapists. Same place as a year ago when they first met. Darcy stays with friends in town. Larry stays in the college dorm. A single room next to a lounge with cinder block walls, plastic chairs, a triangular coffee table, a six-pack of Bud, Styrofoam ice bucket, and three ashtrays, until Darcy adds her scotch.

Larry pours himself a beer and lights up. Darcy pours some scotch over ice. They talk about their jobs. He still owns a clothing factory and fits prostheses. The factory is in Malaysia. He lives in Oregon. Darcy lives in Vermont and works part-time at a health center and part-time at Physicians for Human Rights. At the health center, where she's worked for fifteen years, she molds leg braces. At Physicians, she writes grants to raise money to exhume mass graves—to gather evidence for indicting torturers.

"My boss at Physicians used to be a butcher. Can you believe it?" she says. "One bloody thing after another. And me—a vegetarian. Jesus. The things we all do."

"Yeah, well he's got his reasons, no doubt," Larry says. He pours himself another beer. "Hey, here's to someone beautiful and smart. Remember that." He cocks his glass her way.

She lifts her cup, her eyebrows. He's been so solicitous over the year, has written such kind letters.

I saw the hurt in your eyes, but knowing how hurt people can lash out, timorous shirker that I am, I forbore.

Forbore.

She fell in love with that word as soon as she saw it, rolled it around in her mouth like a large sugar candy. Sucked its juices deep into her throat.

With December darkness and work and snow up to an elephant's ass, you must be goddamn ready to DeeDee outa there. She smiles. She

104

can hear his western twang, his Vietnam cockiness in everything he writes.

"I had to kill people there," he said last summer, almost without opening his mouth. "Fucking blew them apart. Don't tell me about gratuitous violence."

"I don't think people should use violence just to get a rise," she said.

"Why the hell not?" he argued.

But here she is a year later, smiling at the guy. Because he talks about elephants' asses. Thing is, he probably knows how tall an elephant's ass really is. Probably measured himself against one, only he's slightly shorter and trim, taut muscles in his shoulders, his back. She feels them as he gathers her in his long arms.

"Darcy, Darcy." He pulls her in tight. Beer slops over the rim of his glass. Wets her shirt. Her wing bone. "I'm so glad to see you," he whispers over her head, then releases her and stands back, his face paler than she remembers, his nose all cartilage and narrow. Too narrow. She hasn't noticed before.

Darcy feels suddenly timid. She looks down at her hair falling over her shoulders, hitches her purse strap close to her neck. He doesn't know she carries his letters in her purse, reads them over and over.

My heart is with you. I know how it feels. It won't go on forever.

"So. You been writing?" he asks. She writes romances on the side under a pen name.

105

"Only grants for now," she lies. She prefers to think about his healing hands, his blue eyes. And his words, handfuls of them in her bag.

Who doesn't need love? Anyone needs attention. Nurture. A well that needs filling. Yours will. The right guy. He'll come along. I promise you.

She holds onto every word and marvels. He seems to know so much.

The things we don't admit. The way marriage can wear you thin. How we deny the changes, the loss of love, our need for nurture. How we pretend we're fine without it. Affairs don't happen for nothing. Not to people who are smart and vibrant and moral—like you. Not if they get the love they need. So easy to blame yourself for an affair.

Is that what it was? An affair? She thinks back to the woman's unexpected kiss on her forehead. "I'm going home," Darcy had said nervously. But the woman had taken her hand, pulled her in, kissed her on the lips. "I couldn't resist," she wrote Larry. "But why did it happen?" She'd never been with a woman before.

Starving people eat everything you put in front of them.

"How do you know?" she wrote back.

Weeks later, a postcard. (Bison munching hay in a blizzard.)

I wasn't born yesterday. I've seen my share of torment.

"Oh, and with who?" she wrote back.

No answer.

"Remember Ralph Scanner—?" Larry pours himself another beer.

106

Yeah, she remembers. Last summer she danced with him, felt him pressing against her, all the men pressing. Except Larry.

"—Up and died in May." Larry's eyes bug out, bloodshot around the edges. "Sudden cancer. Six weeks. Real shame." He gulps his beer. Gets ready to pour another.

He notices her stare. "I'm fucking tired," he says. "I've come a long way to get here."

"I have too," she almost says. Along with "Your smoke is hurting my eyes. You're drinking too much. We're all alone. Where is everyone?" But she stays quiet. She forbears, pulling her purse close to her, curling her fingers into its soft leather as if by pressing its skin she can touch his words, confirm their reality, their possibility. *The basic things we all need. The touch of a person's hand in ours, a quick smile and squeeze while we wait for someone counting her coupons at the grocery checkout. An evening whispering sweet nothings while we watch fireflies flicker across the fields like stars before our eyes. Crucial small things. Not things we can ever give up. Like a quick one in the kitchen before we race to pick up kids at rehearsal, or a morning in bed with our coffee and the crossword, the steamy summer air wafting over our naked bodies. None of it negotiable. Or reducible. All crucial to, dare I say, happiness.*

But how does he know so much?

Him and his wife, he wrote. His third wife. *You get better as you go along.*

Do you? Darcy wonders. She thinks about the woman's

words. "You're big, not small. You have beautiful hands." Darcy's husband never said such things.

"So you're not romancing?" Larry teases. He steps closer. She smells the day's sweat in his T-shirt.

"No," she says. "My life is pretty boring. Just me and the kids."

"And your friend. You see her?"

Darcy pauses. Tilts her head on purpose. Why is he asking? Didn't she write him? "It's over." In two weeks begun and ended. A year ago. She distinctly remembers writing him in the past tense. "Her touch *drew* me in. It *was* sexy, seductive, pleasurable. The rush *came* on so fast, so full, I simply let go."

She takes a mouthful of scotch, remembers the woman's breast in her mouth. Playful nipple against her tongue. Flesh filling every space. The mother's breast come back again, she remembers thinking, surprised. So this is the magic a man tastes when he covets a woman's breast. Now she knows. This and the thrill of a woman's parted legs.

"But didn't you get my letter?" she asks. Why doesn't he remember *her* words?

Larry drinks down his beer. Shrugs, sheepish.

There's a long pause. Slight blush on his face.

"Just wanted to make sure you're okay now," he says softly. But he bores his eyes into hers as if he knows there has to be more. The rest of the story. What she'll never tell him or anyone. The woman saying, "Now take your fingers," and Darcy complying. Returning the favor. Not at all expecting a woman who wanted penetration. That was what men do. Love between the sheets. They call that lovemaking. Not care and touch during the day, but thrusting at night. So unoriginal. Go get a man, Darcy had wanted to tell her. He'll penetrate you. You watch.

That same night, she told Patrick about the woman. "Kissing and fondling," she said. The same words she wrote to Larry.

."How could you?" Patrick fumed.

"I don't know," she said. "But it's over." She'd never be with a woman again.

"Over?" Patrick's face burned with fury. His eyes narrowed. "How could you?"

Darcy looks into her drink. The ice cubes thin and floating. She thinks about the many times she asked Patrick. Hold my hand. Take my elbow. Lean against me. Let me lean against you.

"It felt good to have something all my own, for a change," she told him. That was the truth.

She watches Larry pour himself another beer. Thinks about the other words she could have told Patrick. *Starving. Curious. Entitled.*

"You need more ice," Larry says quietly. He grabs a handful from the bucket and slides the cubes into her cup, nodding with each addition. *Nurture. Quality. Love.* She watches the scotch rise, feels her body relax.

"And the husband?" Larry asks. He steps closer. "The guy you castrated." He grins. Pats her on the shoulder. "Poor sucker. He cut loose yet?"

Darcy has to chuckle. To anyone else, Larry's comment would seem crass or anxious. But she was the one to mention castration first. Larry's only trying to humor her now. Ease her over. Just like his recent postscript. *Let me tender this one bit of advice.*

Tender. The word like sugar in her mouth. Who these days says tender in this way? A gentleman laying down his coat, offering his hand. His wisdom.

Don't let yourself get bogged down in the arguments about money or things, justice, or even love. Remember, anger and resentment get only you in the end. Whatever you do, don't let the bastard grind you down.

"The divorce is in the works," Darcy says. She tips her glass toward him.

"Good." Larry gives her neck a little squeeze. "But we shall talk later." He nods toward the door. "The party. As promised." He gestures toward the two middle-aged men pushing their backsides against the door, each with a beer in one hand, a six-pack in the other.

"Meet the homeboys, Brad and Willie," Larry announces in a slightly exaggerated tone. He flattens out his palm, first to one, then the other. Darcy recognizes both of them from last summer. Unlike Larry, they're balding and paunchy, but Brad is short. "We love our Sisters" spans his stocky chest, the mountain peaks of

Oregon dark against a sunset sky. Wisps of dirty blond hair sweep his crown. Willie is tall and bony. He wears a sky blue cowboy shirt with pearl snaps. A silver tooled belt.

"Why, hello, Darcy," Brad says in a kind of taunting singsong. He winks at her.

Darcy instantly dislikes him. They've never met before, yet he brandishes her name. So the guys have talked. What have they said?

Willie leans forward to shake her hand. "Glad to meet you, Darcy," he says, his speech slightly slurred. "Me and Larry know each other from way back. He tell you? Even before Nam." His voice is quiet and gentle. "Sure is nice to have a lady in our midst," he adds. For a second he looks at Brad.

"So," Brad rebegins. "You two having a *nice* time?" He raises his eyebrows and looks from Larry to Darcy and back again. He takes a swig of beer. His eye catches the scotch. "Hey, who brought the Glenlivet?" He walks over, picks up the bottle, admires. "My favorite. Mind?" He unscrews the top.

"Wait a sec," Willie says. He sits down, stretches out his legs. "Isn't that Darcy's? Didn't Larry buy that as a present for her?" Willie smiles, skin taut across his jawbone.

Darcy blushes, partly amused, partly pleased to be made the center of attention. Let these guys get their jollies, she figures. Larry'll keep her safe, she knows he will. She watches as he takes them on, snorts and sways back on his heels, the tips of his cowboy boots pointing up like spikes. He stares at the guys, rolls his bottom lip out, big enough to catch anything, and nods real slow as he laughs a quiet one to himself. "Well, actually. I did buy that for Darcy. If I do recall correctly." He pauses. Sucks in from his cigarette. Blows out a thin stream. "In fact"—he sucks again, nods, waits, exhales—"as I recall, you guys were with me, no?" He looks from Brad to Willie and back again. Takes one more draw on his cigarette. Holds the smoke then pops it out in a tidy little knot, his lips a stiff open ring. "Bad memory, Brad? Estrogen-deprived? Nah, wrong sex, I guess." He keeps his mouth hanging open as he stares at Brad. Then he smiles ever so slightly and looks at Darcy. He lets his glee slowly infuse his face.

Darcy holds still. Larry's needling surprises her. It has to be an old joke, she figures. The way men jab at each other when they're drunk. Any woman would be uneasy. Especially among strangers. She'll be fine, she tells herself, swallowing her discomfort.

Brad takes out a cigarette and lights up.

"Mind?" he asks Darcy this time. He gestures toward the bottle. False sweetness lacquers his voice.

She does mind. Everything about him, but she isn't going to make a big deal of it. He's Larry's old buddy from Grant's Pass.

"Sure," she says. "You can have—" she wants to say "a little" but "some" comes out instead. No matter because Brad's already poured his glass full. He sits down, his eyes on his glass, his mouth open, like he's waiting for a sudden revelation. But nothing comes out. He takes a large mouthful of scotch. "Phew." He rattles his head back and forth. "Hits like napalm," he laughs. "Blows your brains, doesn't it."

For a second the other guys laugh too. Then a silence falls. Willie gazes at his belly. Larry sucks his cigarette down to the filter. Darcy flips her hair over her shoulders. Nothing to say or do. Three guys. Heavy drinkers. Her own head spinning now. She ought to leave. But they'll laugh at her, she thinks. Not here, but behind her back, later. Or they'll laugh at Larry. She decides to wait. Be polite, kind. He's been so solicitous. She takes a sip from her plastic cup. Ice against her lips. *Snow up to an elephant's ass.* She smiles. He knows so much.

"Hey. Let me pour you a little more," Larry offers.

"Sure," she says. Let the guys see his care for her. He'll keep her safe. "Just a little, though." She holds out her cup. Larry fills it to the brim. Maybe he isn't listening, she thinks, or just being gracious.

"So nice to see you," he says under his breath. He ruffles her hair. Keeps his hand on her head a few seconds. Forty percent of her body heat capped. She imagines his same big hand fixing limbs. All these guys. Fixing limbs. Probably great at their jobs. But they're goners now. Their debauchery makes her sad. Even Willie, asleep on his chair now, head slumped to one side. The stubble on his cheek looks gray and seedy under the fluorescent lights. Darcy waits for Larry to say something. Make them merry.

She hitches her purse strap closer to her neck.

Brad stands up in a rush. Like she's leaving. "So," he says, his voice oily with anxiety. "You guys have time to *talk*? I mean, me and Willie here don't want to be interrupting anything."

Darcy looks at Larry. Raises her eyebrows. What is it with this guy?

Larry winks. He'll handle this.

"Oh, yeah, we were just *talking*," he mocks. He forms a beak with his right hand and snaps it a few times next to his mouth before he moves it closer to Brad, reaching out as if he might actually snip Brad's shoulder. His thigh. His balls. Brad dances backwards. Darcy giggles, surprised by her own delight. "Ac-tu-al-ly," Larry drags out the word. He looks to see if she's watching. Concocting for her amusement. As if her presence spurs his inventiveness. Darcy feels almost proud to see his performance. "Darcy and I were just talking about households," he drags out his speech. "The kind of thing you wouldn't even know about, Brad, being single such that you are."

Willie sighs heavily. "Larry, cram it, would you?" he mumbles impatiently. He keeps his eyes closed. Swats an invisible gnat.

So he's not asleep. Darcy pauses, wonders. Cram what?

"Why, I was just telling her," Larry says a little more belligerently, staring directly at Brad, "how I'm the cook around my place for all my little women. Make her think I'm a homemaker and I'll have her wrapped up in a jiffy, don't you think, Brad?" He winks at Darcy. Two can play this game. Won't she play, too? They could get Brad together.

"Why, I was just telling her how I made hundred-corner crab balls and Yangchow fried rice with shrimp last night for Beverly," Larry barges ahead. "Red snapper with garlic and black mushrooms for Louanne—her birthday—the night before. And the night before that?" He grins at Darcy. "The night before Beverly's ex came over. It was steak. The guy is still our friend twenty-two years after I stole her from him, and he said he needed meat. So meat it was." Larry lights a new cigarette. "Sometimes guys need red blood on the grill, don't you think, Brad? A little something to get them going, you know, jack them up?" Larry smiles at Darcy. Pulling her leg. She knows it. He's such a damn good liar.

But Brad knows Larry is lying too. Darcy can tell by the glare in his eyes, the beery haze subsiding underneath. "And did you tell her what else you cooked up?" Brad asks. Beads of sweat hang above his lips, parted enough for her to see his little teeth.

Suddenly Larry's face isn't so loose, his volubility no longer so eager.

"I said, 'Did you tell her what else you cooked up?'" Brad repeats, full of derision. He sidles next to Darcy. Presses his shoulder against hers. What does he mean? She waits for Larry to steer him away.

"And just what did you have in mind?" Larry says very quietly.

He crosses his arms over his chest and looks down at Brad. His eyes roam not Brad's face, but his body.

"Your lady, Beverly, for instance," Brad says. His voice has a thin edge. "You tell Darcy what kind of stew she's in now?"

Larry says nothing.

Darcy waits, wonders, eyes the door. She looks at the scotch on the table. His gift. Her favorite. So kind. And expensive. Should she walk out right now and leave it there? What will he think of her then?

"Darcy might want to learn a few things about Beverly's tastes," Brad barrels ahead. "You know. Up front. Before you start spicing things up between you," he says, his voice tauntingly priggish. He reaches over to pat Darcy's shoulder. She recoils. What is he talking about? Spicing up what? She takes a step back just as Larry reaches for her, his arm around her shoulders, and pulls her to him.

"You know, Darcy," Larry says very slowly. "Brad, here, never made it to Nam. Poor guy. Claimed a 4F in training. Physically impaired, he said. Or maybe it was psychological. Or maybe it was something else. What *was* that all about, Brad? You got physical impairments?"

Brad's face grows deep red. Darcy freezes. Whatever these men are hiding, she doesn't want a piece of it. She wants Larry to release her. She pushes away from him, but he pulls her tighter, holds her closer as Brad enunciates his words ever so carefully.

"You tell Darcy what that cunt was doing behind your back?"

Brad must see her eyes widen. Why else would he speak yet louder, his voice edged with saccharine sweetness? "Isn't that what you call your wife of twenty-two years, Larry? Don't you remember? Did you tell Darcy what that *cunt*," he speaks the word with relish, "was doing with another woman? Darcy might like that." He grins triumphantly, takes his index finger, and rams it up the circle he makes with the fingers of his other hand. "Musta been that bloody beef!" Brad guffaws outright. "Jacked her right up. Sure did."

Darcy stands utterly still. What has Larry told them? And why hasn't he said anything about his wife? She looks at him for an explanation, but his face is tight and red, swollen behind his sealed lips. She searches his darting eyes. Tell me, she pleads in a glance. What's going on?

Larry's eyes rove the floor. He talks to no one, everyone. "When she sleeps with a woman, I can call her a cunt," he says, barely opening his mouth. "And when he"—Larry gestures with his chin toward Brad—"a cocksucker, fucks with me, I'll fuck him—"

Darcy doesn't stop to catch his last word. She doesn't take her scotch. Doesn't say goodnight or good-bye or good riddance. She clasps her purse strap and strides across the room, her limbs stiff with the horror of her own held breath. How could he betray her like this? He who forbore, who tendered. She who has taken his words and swallowed them whole, survived on them. Does he think she's a cunt, too? She shoves the door open, rushes down the entryway stairs, and bursts into the night air. She speeds along the path by the building. Through the open window, Brad's voice rings out, nearly braying. "Payback is a mother fucker. At least I learned that much!"

As she walks, the cool air fast upon her, Darcy shudders. She folds her arms across her chest. Wraps her hands around her own flesh. Can you separate a person from his words? She stops and looks back into the lit window, as if she might find her answer in the scathing light. But she isn't there anymore. She's here. Outside. Intact. She glances one more time at the window, as if to be sure. No Larry. Just Brad, buckling at the waist, slapping his thigh, laughing all by himself.

Local Warming

When Quinn calls Sarah to make an appointment because as he puts it, his ass hurts, she tells him right away it's not his ass but his glutes. A week later, when he lies under a sheet on her massage table groaning as she digs her fingers deep into his muscles, pulling at the knotted fibers, she tells him it's her job to force the tissues apart, get the blood moving. She tries to sound matter-of-fact, as if every job, every improvement, involved this pulling, this pain. If only he'd stretch after being up in those trees, she tells him, but she knows he won't. Not him. Too busy running out to The Shanty, the local bar. For a while, she went there, too, sometimes with Quinn, until she couldn't stand it anymore—that dump of a place near the shoreline where seagulls strut along the roof like puffed-up salesmen in double-breasted suits. Sometimes she still imagines the gulls tilting their heads and staring at her. Red beady eyes, as if they could see everything on her. In her. And if she was bleeding—Sarah suspects they knew that, too. Figures

119

they could smell her as they bunched at the cornice and leered.

She's glad she stopped going there, she thinks, as if seagulls were the problem. She prefers being home, she tells herself. So what if she's not in circulation. Didn't she give it a try? She runs her hands down Quinn's freckled leg, moving his energy to his toes and out. At least we're still friends, she tells herself as she rests her hand on his foot a little longer than normal. Twenty years they've known each other, way before their respective divorces.

After she leaves the room, she imagines Quinn lying on the table for a few minutes, listening to the faucet running. Sarah washing her hands. Goddamn her, she can imagine him thinking, unsure whether he's mad at her or at the whole world. All he wants is a woman. A good one like Sarah. Hasn't he told her that? And didn't he encourage her when she worked as a stock broker to get out of that pressure cooker and learn a new trade? Nothing like a divorce to make you think twice. Same as him, he's reminded her. *From car sales to trees. Give me a tree top anytime.*

For a moment she listens, imagining him as he gets off the table and pulls on his pants. Shoves his hands deep inside his pockets, loving how the low corners settle flat. She can picture him jostling his coins, keys, jack-knife, taking out his comb and drawing it through his thinning brown hair, liking how it winnows on either side of his part.

"You okay?" she calls.

She can almost hear his sigh, his complaint. Doesn't she

know it takes longer to dress than undress?

Which isn't to say he's slow. Last week when she called to ask if he could cut apart the weeping willow in the back of her lot—not all of it, just the sixty feet that fell across the neighbor's lawn and stockade fence after a freak October thunderstorm came through—he was there that afternoon, proposing to leave twenty feet of the fat trunk standing. If she left it alone, it'd come back in a year, he said. Big sprouting tentacles, he promised. Then he hesitated. How 'bout we cut a deal, he said. Just a simple trade. You do my ass. I'll do your trees. Strictly professional, okay?

What friends won't do for each other, Sarah smiles to think as she sits at her office desk, waiting for Quinn to emerge, half hoping he'll stop and talk with her a little. She's glad when he pauses in front of her desk, but she can see from the furrow in his brow that something has come up.

"Did Margaret mention anything to you?" he asks. Margaret is Sarah's neighbor of eight years. She runs the food pantry in town, drives dialysis patients to their afternoon appointments, and checks off names at the polls. On some mornings she reads stories aloud at the library, just as Margaret did when her children were little. Quinn knows her for the same reason he knows everybody else in the neighborhood. They've all got trees.

"You couldn't ask me yourself?" Sarah says. She raises her eyebrows playfully and smiles. It's come to this now. This affectionate teasing.

Quinn shrugs. He's not accustomed to forcing himself on people, but he's in a pinch, he says. The guy he's housesitting for wants the house back. Sarah has her place to herself now that Heather's gone off to college. "Thought it might be easier to say no coming from Margaret," he says.

Sarah chuckles. Maybe he's never greeted Margaret in his doorway. Never seen her hovering, asking for donations. For the firemen. The Lions Club. The Booster Club. A sheaf of papers in her chubby hands, her donation bag open and waiting.

"I know it might be awkward," he says, clearly worried about her hesitation. "And I hate to imp—"

"It's fine," Sarah says. They're adults after all. They can handle living in the same house. "You can have the third floor for a month," she says. "Free if you trim the rest of my trees. But no smoking. And take your shoes off at the door, like always. Okay?"

"Sure," Quinn says, wincing slightly. "Like always."

A few days after Quinn moves in, Sarah sees a red bug climbing up the kitchen window. Almost without thinking, she squashes it. Barely gives herself time to look at it. Just takes out the customary Kleenex from her pocket and hunkers down over the bug, squeezing it like a little corpuscle between her fingers. She doesn't even stop to assess the rarity of its design—something she's not seen before. An inverted red V over its back. Probably a variant form of beetle, she figures. What doesn't have a variant form these days?

Local Warming

***

The first week Quinn is there, she doesn't see him much. She isn't sure if he's making himself invisible or just busy. Late at night, when she lies in bed reading, she hears the brush of his footsteps going up the stairs. Clearly in his socks. The smell of cigarettes following him up there, from The Shanty, no doubt. Every morning, she finds his work boots set side by side on the mat, toes pointed perfectly to the wall. As if his boots don't spend every waking hour pointed inward—Quinn being pigeon-toed, though he hates to admit it.

"Ever go see a doctor about it?" Sarah asked last summer.

"Nah," he said. "What's the point? I figure I'm no spring chicken. When I get too old for the pasture, hey, I hope somebody'll just knock me off."

"You don't mean—" Sarah made her fingers like a gun, aimed it at her skull, and pretended to pull the trigger.

Quinn put his head back and laughed. Adams apple rising like a sharp stone. "Only a joke, Sarah," he said. "Jeez, you make it look serious."

Well, it is serious, isn't it? Sarah thinks, listening for the sound of the third floor door closing. She rolls on her side, flips her thick auburn hair out from underneath her, pulls her covers up over her shoulder, and holds them tight around her neck. As if she can keep out the cool night air, or the sound of the seagulls, or the memory of that night on the rocks last summer when Quinn started to take her in his arms. But you don't want him, she says to herself. Remember that.

At the end of the week, when the weather turns oddly warm, Sarah and Quinn sit on the front stoop watching the sunset while the corgies romp around the yard. The female corgi, Mayflower Pride—Pridey for short—is expecting her first litter. She comes right up the stairs when she sees Quinn, rolls over on her back, and splays her legs.

"See, she knows," Quinn says, reaching out to scratch her. He rubs his fingertips around her belly, skirting her nipples, purple and swollen like clams' necks. "A man of touch," he murmurs, leaning slightly toward Sarah, letting their shoulders press. Which is okay, they've decided. Since it isn't going anywhere. Never will.

Sarah likes the way he leans into her, their lanky bodies almost matching. What's a little harmless touch, she thinks. As if she isn't touching people all day.

At the end of the second week, Sarah sees another bug just like the first. She squishes this one, too, though this time she muses a little. Too flimsy for a beetle. Crunches too easily. Maybe it's a mutant firefly. But it's October. Fireflies are July affairs, not autumn seekers. Probably an exotic breed of cockroach, she curses under her breath. Hears her mother's voice echo in her head. That's what happens when you let strangers into your house. They bring in all sorts of bugs. Oh, come on, Mother, she mutters, as if her mother hasn't been dead for years. Quinn's a friend. He's harmless.

Every Thursday, Sarah gives herself the gift of an afternoon to futz. TGIF she calls it. Thank God I Futz. Always glad to be a day ahead of everybody else. Now, if only Carly Padula would hurry up and get dressed, Sarah sighs, thrumming her fingers on the desk. Carly always takes longer to reappear than anybody else. No wonder. Silk panties. Lace bra with underwire. Evan Picone nylons. Full bodice slip. Pearl earrings. Pearl necklace to match. Gold watch. All stacked up nicely on the chair like a little pyramid. One of the Seven Wonders. Do her clients even realize she notices all the little things about them? She understands completely what the piles are about. The illusion, the reassurance—you can put yourself together one layer at a time. She knows exactly what her clients face after she leaves the room. How they pull themselves in a daze from the table, stare in the mirror at the red blotch across their foreheads from the headrest—what will their boss say?—and then at their bodies, sagging breasts, tight buns, flabby legs, blue veins, it doesn't much matter. They all sigh when they gaze at their pile of belongings. Can they pull themselves together in so short a time? They'd so much rather get back on the table and lie there. Forever.

"That's all now," she always whispers when the massage is

over. A signal to remind them time is running again. There is, in fact, life after massage.

But with Carly, she holds back. Carly's an odd case. Right from the start, Margaret said, "My sister-in-law has lung troubles. She needs stimulation. Not cancer, I promise. I'll pay whatever it takes." Carly has recently moved from California to Margaret's house. Carly's husband, an economist, travels a lot. But Carly needs someone to do her treatments, Margaret says. Three times a day she needs someone to knock her chest, shake the phlegm. "That's what I do," Margaret boasts.

Sarah tries to imagine the knocking. Carly is tall, bony, and frail. Her lips are small and delicate, her cheeks pale, her brown bangs clipped in an odd upward arc across her wide brow. "Just massage my back," she said on the first visit, smiling like a china doll, looking down at the floor as she spoke, just as she does now.

"Sorry I'm so slow," she whispers as she slides into the chair next to the desk, her watch and shoes still in her hands. "I tried to be fast, I really did, but as you know," she smiles without looking up, "it takes time to dress." She sets her shoes on the floor then focuses on her watch, which she drapes across her wrist, fingering the clasp like a praying mantis.

"So, when do you think I should come back?" she asks, her voice soft.

Sarah takes a deep breath. Such an odd woman, this one. "The usual," she says. "As long as it helps, come."

Local Warming

"You are so kind," Carly says. She snaps the watch closed. "I'm assuming Margaret is—"

"Yes," Sarah answers, all the while staring at the flat bridge between Carly's eyes, a shallow almost concave place. If you didn't know better, you'd think she'd had an operation to scoop out the bridge section and put it somewhere else.

Sarah loves the quiet that settles over the office when she closes up. Even more, she relishes the feel and look of the fresh white sheet on the massage table. She folds the top down a few inches, runs her hand along the new crease. Today, she catches herself musing. Suppose she turns down one corner. Will someone appear during the night? Be there to greet her in the morning? Such a silly thought. Does she want that? She lets the sheet dangle. It reminds her of long floppy arms. She closes the window, turns off the radio, switches on the answering machine, and pulls the door snug behind her. The brass bolt slides easily into place.

Glad to be free, she saunters the half mile home along the streets of Noank, past the tall clapboard houses with their widow's walks. It's odd, this fall, how warm it's been. She imagines ice caps melting in the North Pole. She knows she should be worried about these signs of global warming. But she loves the warmth. And the smell of the sea as it mixes with the nuttiness in the air. The dry leaves she kicks and crunches all the way home. It's been so long since rain. But things don't feel parched this year, she realizes, thinking about the warmth in her house. How nice it is to have Quinn around. Just enough company to make her feel more welcoming, she thinks as she rounds the corner and sees Margaret sitting on her front porch.

"I knew I could catch you here!" Margaret calls out, her voice a mixture of glee and triumph.

Sarah stops. Margaret is wearing one of her baggy house dresses. Her short gray hair curls around her head. No sheaf of papers. No zippered bag.

"I just want to thank you," Margaret calls out again, beckoning with her hand for Sarah to keep coming, as if she can feel Sarah's urge to find a different front porch. "To thank you for all you're doing," she calls out. "It's so reassuring to know there are neighbors who are genuinely, well, you know, genuine!"

Sarah stands a moment longer, wondering what Margaret really wants. Another favor, no doubt. A room for Carly, too? Sarah would be lying to say she hasn't anticipated such a prospect. The three of them together. Quinn drifting toward Carly. Carly welcoming his embrace. And him, eager to help her, to take her in his arms, to—. Oh, leave it, she admonishes herself, remembering how polite Quinn is. How tentative. "Could I kiss you?" he'd asked that night. "I'd rather not," she'd told him, unable to stop thinking about his wanting to be put out to pasture. Who would want that? But still she wonders. What would a kiss have been like with him? Would it have changed everything else? She looks up at Margaret, ready to hear the request. *A little crowded in my house. But you, you have so much space. Can Carly come here?*

"I'll be right with you," Sarah says, surprised at how much she's really not in a mood to deal with Margaret today, at how much she just wants to go into her own house, get settled, let the dogs out, and enjoy the quiet, the warmth inside. She takes a breath, knowing if she goes to get her empty garbage can from the street, she'll have time to figure out her response to Margaret. I know this seems inconceivable to you, she'll say, but I really like my house to myself. I like knowing I'm alone. No need to tell Margaret she's actually enjoying Quinn's quiet presence. His warm body at her breakfast table, leafing through the paper. The other night, even the way he sliced an onion gave her pleasure. So thin and perfect. His fingertips perched right close to the knife, the vegetables lined up like soldiers before the sauté. "I know it's fall," he said, "but here's pasta primavera."

As it ends up, Margaret just wants to know if Sarah can continue the treatments for Carly. It looks like Carly is going to stay longer than she planned, Margaret says. Apparently Margaret's husband, Keith, who works the graveyard shift at Electric Boat, has mixed feelings about it, but she's family, Margaret says. You can't exactly kick out family, can you? Or friends, she adds at the last second, giving Sarah a curious kind of look.

No sooner does Sarah get settled at her kitchen table with tea and crackers than she sees another of those red bugs creeping up the window pane. This time, she kills it very gently, squishing it slowly so as to preserve its features. When she unfolds her Kleenex, she studies the bug. No pinchers. A long body. Wings that fold over each other to make that delicate red V. Spindly legs that on a lobster she would gladly rip off and suck. She carries the Kleenex to her desk and pulls out her insect book. There between Squash Bugs and Stink Bugs, she finds her specimen. Eastern Boxelder Bug. *Leptocoris trivittatus*. She reads the Latin slowly, like a priest chanting to the congregation. *In Domino confido. Leptocoris trivittatus*. Well, at least this isn't an exotic breed of cockroach, she says to herself. (You see, Mother, Quinn is clean. Harmless.)

But having never seen these bugs before, still she worries. Is this something that will eat away at her foundation? Does she have an infestation of some sort? She reads on. "The Eastern Boxelder Bug does little damage to trees," the book says, "though it does cause deformities and blemishes in fruit." No problem, Sarah thinks, relieved forsythia bushes line her back yard alongside the weeping willow. Nothing like the apple trees at Margaret's house. But why so many of these bugs, now, pressing at her panes? Her eye catches the asterisks at the bottom of the page. "In autumn," the text reads, "huge swarms of females can be seen near buildings, looking for a place to overwinter." Huh, she smiles. Imagine. These females have chosen her house. How quaint, she thinks, deciding she won't kill them anymore.

Local Warming

***

When Quinn comes home that night, a little earlier than usual, she asks him about the bugs. Has he seen them?

"Oh yeah," he says. "Them and the *Eranis tilaria*. They're all over the place these days." He fills the kettle with water. His usual now. A nice cup of hot tea with milk and honey to send him off to bed.

"*Eranis tilaria?*" Sarah is surprised to hear these words coming out of Quinn's mouth, but of course, as a tree man, he would know his bugs.

"The linden loopers," he says. "You know. Those light brown moths you see everywhere?"

"Ah, yes," Sarah says, as if she's also seen them in swarms. "Are they something special?"

Quinn laughs. "Nah," he says. "Usually they're dead by now. Cold snap gets them. But this year. Well, you know. Nothing's dying this year." He grins as he starts up the stairs, a little bounce to his step. He's been at Margaret's for dinner, with Carly and the gang, he says cheerfully. Eggplant Parmigiana.

"But do the bugs eat things?" Sarah calls up after him.

Her voice echoes in the stairs.

"Do they eat things?" she calls again, unable to tell if he's closed the door already.

"Hey, look," Sarah says to Quinn the next morning, pointing to the *New London Day*.

"Hang a minute, will you?" he says. He's on his way to Margaret's to borrow milk.

Sarah reads the article without him. "Balmy Weather Draws Moths Out." What a coincidence. Right here in front of her—all the information she needs. "The winter-moths," the article says, "technically *Eranis tilaria*, aren't the kind of moths that sneak into homes to munch wool. They're the males, looking for suitors. If you look closely in the trees," the article continues, "you can see the little gray wingless females crawling around looking for a date."

Heavens, Sarah thinks. All this life teeming around her. And here she is, in the middle of it. A host.

By the time Quinn comes back from Margaret's, Sarah is getting ready to leave.

"Did you want to show me something?" he says, coming into the front hall. His cheeks seem suddenly very red to her. As if he has a fever. Is he okay, she wants to know. Does he have a temperature?

"Oh?" He strides over to the mirror by the door and gazes. Indeed, they're red, he says like a revelation. He pats them as if they were cold. "Just stacking firewood," he says. "Big pieces I cut up yesterday. Left them on Margaret's walk. Oh, and I did Carly's treatment, too," he adds, as if it were nothing.

"You did what?" Sarah asks. She stops in the doorway.

"Her treatment. You know, for her lungs," he says over his shoulder. He's on his way into the kitchen to put the milk away. Sarah knows he'll have a dollop in his coffee first. She can almost hear him lifting the mug and drinking it down.

He hums a little as he comes back, not looking at her as he flings open the closet door and grabs his jacket. It's supposed to get cooler later on. Does she know? But she'll be indoors all day, he says, humming a little more, pretending, it seems, not to notice the way she's still standing in the doorway, her mind suddenly caught by a prospect she hasn't seriously considered before. How Carly's body might receive his touch, her bony sternum softening under his fingertips. Maybe Sarah's not the only one who can give solace. The realization makes her heart seem to seize up, but she's not about to let him see her panic.

"I guess that's pretty cool," she says, trying to sound upbeat and merely curious as she wonders aloud, "But what does that mean, 'Do her treatment'?"

"Oh, I just pound her chest in a few places while she lies down," Quinn says, as if it were nothing. "Front and back." He hammers the air a little. "Margaret trained me," he adds. "I'm pretty good at it."

"I'll bet you are," Sarah says a little too quickly. "And does Margaret watch?" She can't stop herself from asking.

Quinn pauses to stare at her, his puzzlement clear. What

an odd question. As if the three of them have something kinky going on. "What do you think?" he asks. And then, before she can answer, "Wouldn't that be a little bizarre?"

"Oh, forget it," Sarah says, fluttering her hand in quick dismissive jitters. "That came out all wrong. I'm sure you're great with her. Whatever you do!" Her words come out in an exasperated rush. "Now, if you'll excuse me, I'm off to work." She strides down the walk, shaking her head, marching on as if she didn't know Quinn was still standing there, staring after her. She's half relieved when he clears his throat. Maybe he wants to tell her Carly doesn't even get undressed.

"Hey," he calls out. "You want me to walk the dogs at noon, today?"

"Sure," she calls over her shoulder, trying to sound grateful. "That would be perfect. Thanks."

When Carly's treatments become a regular part of Quinn's routine, Sarah tells herself it's no big deal. It only means Quinn is around the house a little more in the morning while he waits for Margaret's kids to leave for school so the house is empty.

"But isn't Keith home by then?" Sarah asks one morning. She's starting to wish Quinn had his original schedule, leaving her a little more time alone in the morning.

"I guess not," Quinn says, cracking his eggs into the fry pan. "Maybe he has another job. Or maybe he goes out for breakfast—

to The Shanty." He grins. "How would I know?"

Sarah smiles. The nicest part of the new schedule is that Quinn seems a lot happier and healthier these days—no more drinking or late nights. No cigarette smoke either. She figures that has to do with Carly. Pound a person's chest long enough and it probably makes you think twice. Nowadays when she gets home from work, she often finds Quinn, Carly, and Margaret sitting around her kitchen table having tea and chatting. Carly has a new job at the library and is full of stories about the place. Margaret babbles about her children. Quinn is usually making supper—for Sarah, too. He's done the grocery shopping. Walked the dogs. "All I ask," she says, "is for peace and quiet on Thursday afternoons and the weekends."

"That's easy," Quinn says as he flips his eggs. "We'll shift our time to earlier on Thursdays. That way, we won't be in your hair."

For a second, Sarah thinks she's heard him wrong.

"You'll what?" she asks. She stares at him, unable to believe he would bring a woman over to her house, astonished when he tells her he and Carly often do the midday treatment over here. Apparently Keith doesn't like the coughing in the other house.

"But you never asked if it was okay," she says. Her voice catches in her throat. "I mean," she pauses, trying to figure out the most obvious reason why it's unacceptable, so as to sound less picky. "If people see you leading some strange woman into my house, they'll all think I'm—"

135

"Oh, they all know why she comes," Quinn says quickly. "That's not a problem. It's all in the neighborhood. And since you aren't home, there's nobody here to bother. The house is quiet, empty. Enviable, Margaret would say."

Sarah sits still for a moment. Clearly he doesn't understand something crucial. Something she didn't think she needed to tell him. Not simply that he's a guest in her house, but that it's her house.

"How can you bring a woman into my house?" she asks, making her outrage clear.

"Jesus, Sarah." He thrusts his fork down and shoves his hands, palms up, in front of her, as if he expects her to lean over and check them for dirt in his lifelines. "It's not like we're fucking or anything. It's all very clean, Sarah."

"But it's my house!" she insists. How could he, her friend, do this?

"So, okay, I'm sorry," he says, full of exasperation. "I should have asked. But really," he pauses as if he knows he's crossing a line, "What harm gets done? I mean, it's not like she's spreading germs. And there's nobody else here to annoy. You have to admit that!"

Sarah can't believe what she's hearing. "I need to know the house is mine," she says, feeling her heart race. "That's all."

"Fine," Quinn snaps, getting up to rinse his plate. Without another word, he gets his coat and heads out the door. Sarah can almost hear him thinking, if you'd given me what I wanted in the first place, this would be a lot easier now.

The next week, when Carly calls to cancel her regular Wednesday afternoon appointment—the library needs her, she says, sorry to cancel at the last minute—Sarah is glad. She fills the slot with Mandy Cristiano and heads out the door to work. The forecast is for driving rain turning to ice. So much for global warming, she thinks. Quinn calls after her that he'll be doing Nan and John Miller's trees today, right up the street. Does she want him to walk the dogs at noon? Things are better between them now that he's apologized again and begun to look for a new place to live.

By one o'clock, the rain has already begun and the temperature is dropping. Sarah can hear the ping against the windows in the massage room. During the next hour, the rest of her clients call to cancel their appointments. So, fine, Sarah thinks. She'll have the afternoon off. Not a bad way to spend a rainy day—home with tea, the newspaper, a book. As she walks home under her umbrella, she passes the Millers'. Quinn's van is still in the driveway. She wonders if he's up in the trees. They'll be slick. Even treacherous. But he'll be careful, she knows.

She sighs with pleasure when she gets inside her house, shakes off her wet clothes, and hangs them up. She sorts the mail—a pile for her and a pile for Quinn. She wonders how it will feel not to have him there anymore. She puts on a wool sweater and some slippers to stave off the chill in the house. Too soon to have the furnace turning on automatically. She puts on the tea kettle. How nice this unexpected free afternoon feels. On the sly, like a criminal in her own house. Does it get more delicious than that? She listens to the clicking of ice on her windows. She hasn't seen her bugs in a long time. That's a relief. No infestation after all. And the dogs are quiet in the basement. Sleeping, no doubt, after Quinn has walked them. Bless them—and him—she thinks, not at all eager to make a tour of the neighborhood in this lousy weather.

With her tea and honey, she cozies into a chair at the kitchen table and starts leafing through the newspaper, so immersed in her reading she barely hears the footsteps coming down the stairs. Even when they register in her brain, she doesn't react. So many years of hearing footsteps. Maybe it's Quinn home for a nap, she thinks idly. The rain. The cold. He too would want to come in.

But there's something different about the steps. Not one person but two. A double tapping. More calmly than Sarah would have imagined (so they've been fucking after all), she prepares herself to see her visitors. Quinn first. Then Carly. Oddly, she doesn't feel angry, but curious. Even embarrassed. Not for her, but for them. Like school children caught red-handed. She imagines Carly tiptoeing down in her frail way, her hand draped in Quinn's with the same self-effacing meekness she shows each week at the office as she lays her watch across her wrist. Her fingertips perched on his palm like a bird at a feeder. How Quinn will covet that touch. This chance to guide a woman. Step here. Not there. Easy does it. One tread at a time. As if you can lead a woman to Paradise not in one fell swoop, but by these incremental downward steps.

Sarah stays very still. She waits for the figures to come into view. She feels almost like laughing, this is finally so ridiculous. So utterly predictable. Grown people acting like children. She half expects to see her own daughter slinking down the stairs with one of her boyfriends in tow.

"Why, hello, there," Quinn says quietly as he comes to where the stairs turn toward the kitchen. From his sheepish tone, Sarah doesn't need to look to see if he's blushing.

"Oh, hi," Sarah says, eyes on the newspaper. She keeps flipping the pages. Quinn comes forward into the kitchen. He's alone, but Sarah knows someone else is there. She can feel the hovering. Come out, she wants to call to Carly. You might as well come out. I won't bite, she thinks, just as Margaret steps out from around the corner. Margaret with her blouse puffed out on one side. Her short gray hair mussed. Her lips drawn tight. For a moment Sarah only stares as she feels a surge of heat roar through her body, as if Margaret were the boiler switch herself.

Sarah gazes at Quinn. At the fire in his eyes. Then at Margaret.

At the slow-blooming defiance on her red face. Her thick arms folded not so much across her chest as under her sagging boobs. This is what Quinn wants?

"No, no," she almost turns to him and says. Suddenly it's all so clear. "You don't want her anymore than she wants you, or *I* want you," she thinks as she feels a pinch to her heart. A moment of sadness. One man down, a million to go. But at least she understands now. It isn't each other they want, but want itself.

Remember Love

The first time I danced with Mark, I knew he would take me somewhere if I would let him. We were in dance class. Not choosing partners, just rotating around the circle. Lots of men, but none like Mark, who even before the music began stood before me slightly crouched and bouncing, snapping his fingers on the off-beats, waiting while the saxophones surged, the bass pulsed deep into our bones. *Two four six eight*. He added a small as if unconscious shimmy when the beat came back to one, listening for the first set of phrases to finish—*five six seven eight*—before he lowered his hand in front of me. One definite downward motion. Here now. Take this. His eyes lit up like a magician's laying out a deck of cards in front of an expectant crowd. Yes, yes. You there. This one's for you.

When I reached out, instantly I felt his pressure, his push cueing me back, his pull tugging me forward, the trumpets going wuuaah wuuaah. *Two three*. A slight whip around. Come circle next to me, baby. His body talking. He pulled me close along his right side and tucked me under his arm. Together we triple-stepped, *seven and eight*, both of us listening as the trumpets notched up in harmony this time. A new group of phrasings. He trailed me back. Planted his hand on my right hip, his fingers pressed against my bone. Not afraid, this man. His left arm ahead of us like a crossbeam, he guided me sideways and swiveled my hips, *swivel, swivel*, as he whispered under his breath—*one two three four*—we were only learning—until he bent his knees like a skater about to launch his partner into the air. Only we were in jeans and he was gentle as he let me go. "Ah," he said, as he saw the ease of my turn away then back, our arms elastic, *seven eight*. The trumpets blaring. So easy to follow. He didn't stop when the teacher cut off the music, but took me for one more turn until we were square with each other. "Who needs practice?" he whispered into my ear.

When he grinned, I saw two small black teeth alongside the other white ones. Worn down, skinny and uneven, like spires in the Badlands. From an injury? Childhood? Bad teeth when he was born? He didn't seem to care.

By the time the lessons ended in December, Mark and I had already entered a few Jack and Jill dance competitions. We'd gone out to Pottstown first, to a real dance place where we could practice our moves, get out the jitters, pretend people were watching, judging. For a guy who seemed so quietly focused in class, Mark surprised me by his quick invitation. Would I climb Mt. Adams with him next month, maybe traverse the Presidential Range? In New Hampshire, in the White Mountains. He told me he even took his mother up there once for a Christmas present when he was in college. Bundled her up like a kindergartner and hiked her up Mt. Adams to Gray Knob, the caretaker's hut. "For years she talked about the stubby pines mounded with snow. Glittering like diamonds," he said. "Her words," he added quickly. "Cliché, I know. But she loved it." Then he showed me the picture of snow angels. "Me and Mom," he said. "Her idea. Funny, huh."

Or more likely weird. A forty-eight-year-old man who carries a picture of his mother tucked in his wallet. Not even her, but a snow-wrinkled impression of her from thirty years ago. I should have run the other way. Thing is, I like snow angels. Even more, I liked his warmth. His quick smile. The lift of his voice when he said, "Funny, huh." As if he truly relished being caught between wonder and surprise.

He showed me that photo on our first official date at the Ballroom on High. He had roses for me that night. Peach and yellow.

Brian used to bring me roses, too. Red ones.

For our first competition, a week before Thanksgiving, Mark wore saddle shoes. A purple vest with suspenders. I wore a red tank top with black leggings. "Let them see your hips," he urged when I put the top on.

"Big old hips," I said, letting the shirt hang.

"Nice hips. I like them. I love them," he said that night in bed.

"Be careful with that word," I said. "Don't use it for nothing."

"I love your curls, too," he said.

"Don't throw it around."

"So soft. Like your breasts," he said, brushing his fingertips under the magical curve, he called it. Where flesh meets rib. "The perfect place," he said, taking his time.

"But why were you never married?" I asked afterwards, lying tight in his arms. I knew it was none of my business, but I needed to know. No mistakes this time.

"Got me," he said shrugging.

"No, really."

"Look who's talking."

"But I was married. For twenty-three years."

"And then divorced—"

"You're not answering my question."

"I'll bet you can't do this," he said. He reached up to my ear, pulled out five gold coins, and balanced them on his fingertips. "Pick one," he said.

When I first saw Mark dance, I figured he was a skier or a runner. He learned much quicker than the rest of us to bounce with the beat, not up but down, down deep into the floor, our teacher said. Take the music into your body—*seven EIGHT*—the teacher counted as the trumpets crescendoed with their skittery blues. Mark, six feet tall and wiry, grinned as he bounced like someone in a starting gate warming up before the gun.

When we headed up Mt. Adams, he had that same bounce in his legs. "Come catch me," he teased, running in his snowshoes. "Follow me. Your fearless leader." He broke our steps up the snowy path, divvying out semi-sweet chocolate squares, which I sucked on the roof of my mouth, relishing the sweetness. "You'll love it. I promise," he said, not even looking back to see if I was following.

"And suppose I don't?" I called up after him, only half-joking. I'd never told him about rafting with Brian. Brian who loved rafting. Who said I would love it, too. One summer we drove from Scranton to Glacier without stopping. We couldn't get there fast enough for him. Such fun, he promised. But the crashing water terrified me. The lubberly boat felt as if it might break in two. My neck jerked. My bones snapped. Or so it seemed.

"Oh, but you will," Mark called back. He was on a steep section. Snow piled all around him. The trees sharp against the blue sky. "Because it's beautiful up here—and I *know* you," he added. But for a second he stood and stared at me, his head tilted, brow creased, as if maybe I wasn't the person he thought I was after all.

145

"Hey, let's go," I said, not liking the look of that stare. I never asked my other question. *When is it my turn to lead?* I could just imagine his answer. *Who's stopping you?*

All the way up the mountain we munched peanuts and raisins. Gulped water while it was still liquid. Around noon, we burst through the trees and started along the windswept ridge, trading snowshoes for crampons under a sky so blue it made my eyes ache. I'd never been in crampons before. I cinched the straps tight, fearful it was all an illusion, this walking on ice. Not even steep ice. But that wasn't the point. It was slippery. Isn't that one thing we all know in life—ice is slippery? Gingerly, I stepped forward, waiting to slide back. But the crampons bit instantly, snugged deep with each step, except where the rock lay hidden under the glaze. "Don't move one foot unless you've planted the other," Mark said. "You know, like this." He started counting. *One two.* But instead of walking, he did a quick spin. "Stop worrying," he said, looking at me. "I'll keep you safe. I promise. Look." He pulled out a thick line from his backpack, looped it around my waist, tied a figure eight knot, stretched me thirty feet behind him, took out his ice axe, and planted it with every step. Breathless, I kept walking. I could be Spiderman, climbing walls, I thought. I could go anywhere. Look Ma, no hands, I wanted to call out to the heavens.

Halfway up the ice field, Mark suddenly stopped. I stopped,

too, careful to keep the line taut between us. What was the problem?

"Just look at this snow!" he called out. Off to our right, not a crevice or boulder broke up the glittering expanse. He started galumphing up the slope. No longer in front but up above, he turned and began to haul me in hand over hand. "Watch out for the crevasses—and the polar bears," he teased as he saw me sink up to my thighs. I leaned back a little, eager to feel his pressure. The snow squeaked. When I got close, I waited for him to reach out, grab my hand, pull me in.

But suddenly the line went slack. "No, don't," I said, seeing him crouch. I could tell he meant to take me in his arms, put me in a sweetheart turn. But he would tangle our crampons in the line. Trigger our slide off the mountain. "I don't have the bal—"

He lunged forward and knocked me into the deep powder. Flipped on his back and pulled me so I lay on top of him. Blew the snow out of my hair, his breath warm on my face. "Snow angels," he said grinning. "We have to make snow angels."

When we sat up to dust off our jackets and hats, in the distance, I could see Mt. Adams and beyond that Mt. Washington, the whole ridge perfectly clear, the sky a brilliant blue, the sun warm on my face. "Hey, let's do the whole traverse," I said. "We don't have to stop at Adams if you don't want."

So we kept going. Mark had told me one night as we lay in bed that when you hike up Mt. Adams, there are two cabins just before tree line. One is Gray Knob, where a lone caretaker keeps the winter fire going. Eight climbers can snuggle into skinny bunks and be assured of warmth. First come first served. About a half mile away, almost on the ridge, stands the other cabin. "Right here," he'd said, pressing near my armpit. He hadn't told me the other cabin was merely a shell of itself. Two rooms. An old kitchen with sawed-off pipes from the cistern, its windows long ago boarded up on the outside. On the inside broken mullions spired from the frame.

Nor did he tell me that halfway through our traverse, a sudden storm might sweep over the mountains, the blinding snow and cutting winds making it impossible to see the cairns or find our way along the ridge. For a long time, it seemed, we huddled on the leeward side of a cairn, my fingers and toes slowly freezing, despite my gloves, my socks. I laced my arms tight across my chest, my gloved fingers snug in my armpits. *Right here.* I tried to calm myself. We would be fine. Anyone can be caught in a storm. It will pass. But Mark knew we needed to press on, and so he did, managing to find by compass each successive cairn, each tall and icy pile of rocks a haven to me as I waited to hear his voice urging me forward. He didn't dare leave each new cairn he found to come back and fetch me, in case he couldn't find it again, but called out to me, this way, you can do it, you'll be fine, until finally in the trees, we were in front of the warm cabin, Gray Knob. We didn't expect to find it boarded up or locked.

By the time we went the additional half mile to the other cabin, it was almost dark, but at least the storm was letting up. We plunged through the fresh snow, breathed easier when the door opened. For a moment I just stood staring at the wrecked remains of the place, grateful to be out of the storm, but my fingers were so numb I almost couldn't take off my gloves or my boots.

"Why did they destroy the windows?" I asked shivering in the boarded-up darkness, staring at the few glass corners still in place, like a photo album waiting.

"Probably needed firewood," Mark said, turning on his headlamp, his breath steaming. "Probably whacked them with their ice axes." He swung his axe as if he needed to show me how. "Probably the same guys who did that," he said, walking me into the other room and pointing his headlamp at the hacked base of an old pump organ in the corner. A pile of ivory keys and pearl-headed stops lay on the floor alongside.

"God knows why they didn't burn those, too," he said, kneeling so I could sit and put my frozen feet and hands on his warm belly. "Probably knew the ivory smelled bad." He winced as my skin touched his. "Probably desperate for warmth." He kept talking as he started to rub my toes, my fingers. "We'll get your circulation going," he said. "Then we'll light my camp stove. You can hold your fingers near the flame."

"But have you really smelled burning ivory?" A silly question,

I realize now. I should have asked about frostbite. Was it okay to heat my fingers or rub them if we were going out into the cold again? But I was a potter. I knew the smell of singed hair from Rakú firing, and the smell of burned flesh, too. For some reason, I needed to know. Had he really smelled ivory?

"Does it really matter?" he said. Then before I could reply. "Yes, once."

"You mean, you—?" I gestured toward the hacked up organ, pulled my fingers away a little.

He looked at me puzzled. "Who, me?"

My fingers throbbed as they began to thaw.

Throbbed as I put them near the flame, too, until the fire sputtered out and Mark, going to get his second fuel canister from his pack, discovered it was empty. Could he have forgotten to fill it? But he never forgets, his voice urgent as he packed us up and headed us down the back of the mountain, an easier path through the woods, even with the heavy snow, the blue blazes on the trees pulling us like magnets, one tree to the next, the feeling coming back in my toes. His socks, an extra pair. Warm and thick. (Why hadn't I thought to bring an extra pair?) But I could do this, I said to myself, over and over. I would be all right. I wouldn't waste my energy getting nervous or mad. I wouldn't ask—didn't he know storms could come up suddenly?—anymore than I would ask, why had I followed him up here in the first place? I took his hand as he reached to help me down the steep parts. No point in getting mad.

But how could he have forgotten the fuel? And why were my fingers feeling cold again, then numb, as if they weren't even there?

The last time I sat with Brian was eight years ago. We were in his car. He'd asked me to come for a drive. Said he'd pick me up at the house so we could discuss how to help the boys with the separation. But a mile from the house, he pulled onto the shoulder and stuck out his hand.

"I want my ring back," he said. "Not the gold one. You can melt that one down. But the diamond. It cost me a lot of money. It's mine."

How quickly I began to slip the rings off. I didn't want his damn old rings anyway.

At first they slipped easily, until I got to my knuckle, swollen or calcified, it seemed. As I twisted and tugged, trying not to show the pain, Brian kept his foot on the gas pedal. When the rings finally slipped off, he thrust out his hand, his palm open and eager. I reached out, too, ready to place the rings just where he wanted them. But in that second, something made me pull back, curl my fingers around my rings, and tell him he couldn't have them. They were mine. A gift to me.

"Get out," he said as I put them in my pocket.

I didn't slam the door behind me. I closed it gently, pushing to make sure it latched, never showing how I was trembling as he drove away, yelling at me through the glass, as if I could hear, or cared to hear, his words.

The first time I met Mark's mother was early December, a month before our Mt. Washington climb. On the drive over to the nursing home, Mark spewed forth almost uncontrollably. "If you so much as press against the doors," he warned, "I mean, if you even just let your fingertips settle on the handle and push slightly to open it without first dialing the combination, you'll set off every buzzer in the place. Then the nurses—you won't know they're nurses, because they're dressed like the rest of us—will come running, along with the old people. Not just the ones who'll come over when they hear the buzzer and chastise you. Maybe even laugh at the alarm as if the joke's on you." He winced. "But the ones who'll stand there tottering with their heads drooping, looking at that open door as if they know something's out there, if only they could remember what. Those are the ones that'll get you."

As he spoke, he kept his eyes fixed on the highway, the steering wheel tight in his hands, his knuckles yellow against his skin.

"Maybe you don't want me to come," I said quietly. The harshness in his voice surprised me. Just the night before, in a whisper, he'd pressed his fingertips onto my heart and said, "You know you're in love by this, Becca. Not this." He'd touched my head.

He kept staring straight forward at the road—had he even heard me? His face and eyes were so still, it was as if he were watching not something outside, but inside. In his head. Or was it in his heart? A sequence I might never see.

"No, no," he said after a time, his voice distant. "Mom really wants to meet you. She can't believe you dance with me. That I'm a dancer. Funny, huh."

Only this time his words sounded tight and pained. For a moment, I worried. Maybe that expression I loved in him was just a nervous tic. Maybe there'd be no wonder after all. No surprise. No taking our time.

"But, really, I can sit in the car and wait," I said, suddenly wondering if I'd made a mistake. Maybe this was all premature, my meeting his mother. And yet I wanted to meet her, though not for the reasons I'd given him. I hated to admit how old school I'd become, thinking it wise to see a man with his mother, as if the way they interacted might assure me. He was the right choice. I was the right choice. And if I liked her, maybe that would mean something too. I never spoke about my deeper worry. Did Alzheimer's run in his family? Did I want that in my future, a man with Alzheimer's to care for, to ache for? Follow your heart, not your mind, he'd said. But what about my choices, I wanted to say back. My careful and deliberate choices.

"But I don't want you to sit in the car," Mark said. "And *you* don't want to, either. Remember how eager you are to meet her?"

He reached over to pat my thigh, his hand banging against the bag of Chinese food on my lap, as if he'd forgotten it was there. He smiled then patted the top of the bag instead. "Just what the doctor ordered," he said. He looked at his watch. We were on time. His mother would be so pleased. Everything would be fine.

But I could still feel his tension as we drove on, his knuckles white as he gripped the steering wheel, guiding us between the whizzing cars on the Schuylkill Expressway. In the silence, I couldn't stop thinking about our last dance competition. We made it all the way to the finals—the second-to-last couple to be tapped on the shoulder, the signal we were out. "The follower hesitated a few times," the judge whispered as she sent us off the floor.

After a while, I reached out to turn on the radio.

"Could we not?" Mark said, intercepting my hand.

"But Mark—"

"Could we not!" he said so sharply I drew my hand back and held still. It's only music, I wanted to say, thinking how much he loved music. How much we both loved music.

"Look, my mother knows your name," he turned suddenly to say to me, as if we'd been arguing all along.

I sat still. What was he talking about?

"My mother *knows* your name," he said louder, panic in his voice.

"Of course," I answered, hoping to calm him. "I'm sure she knows—"

"I've told her your name countless times. Becca, Becca, Becca," he whispered sharply toward the windshield as if he could carve my name into the glass. "I just want you to know she might forget who you are," he said, still staring out the windshield. "If she does—" he swallowed hard—"don't be hurt."

When we arrived at St. Mary's Alzheimer's Center, Deborah was already in the small dining room Mark had reserved for us. Through the plate glass window, we could see her sitting at the table. She was tall and lean like Mark, only her hair was curly and white. In her hands, she toyed with a sprig of dried hydrangea. She must have plucked it from the centerpiece. I wondered how long she'd been sitting there. Who'd pushed her in so close? Would she know who we were?

For a second I held my breath as Mark opened the door. Instantly she turned, her eyes bright with anticipation. "Mark," she called, reaching out to greet him. He strode into the room with a bounce to his step, leaving me at the door, as instructed. Introductions befuddle her, he'd cautioned. Take your time. I watched and waited as he pulled out her chair then kissed her on the cheek. She took his hand, pulled it close to her skin. I felt myself relax at this tenderness, even when she suddenly let go and looked down—Mark's coat had swept the dried hydrangea onto the floor. Quickly she bent over to pick it up, her hand trembling as she set it on the table. But this was fine, I said to myself, seeing

Mark's lips pull tight as she started dithering with the stem, trying to get it to point right at her, it seemed. She just needed to get settled, I said to myself, remembering my own mother's care in setting up her room at the nursing home, her determination to get everything in the right place. People need time to get settled, I reminded myself. Especially old people.

It was lovely to see how Mark gave her a little time before he touched her shoulder. "Mom," he said. She looked up a little startled. "I want you to meet my friend—." He paused before he said my name slowly and deliberately, as if to land it right on her lips.

As promised, I took my time coming in and reaching out for her hand, her fingers thin but strong. "How do you do— Deborah," I said, wondering if she—or he—heard the care I also took to let her name crystallize in the air, as if I could hang it right in front of her as permanently as she might hang my own. She smiled and nodded. Yes, everything would be fine, I thought, even when she suddenly glanced down again, grabbed at her cardigan, and fumbled at the clasp on the end of the string of pearls holding it together. The pinchers had come undone. She pulled at the chain, trying to stretch it across the bulky sweater she also wore underneath. "She wants to wear everything at once," Mark had said. "She's afraid she's going to lose things. They lock up her stuff now. Don't be alarmed."

"Mom," Mark said quietly. He stepped closer. "Would you

like some help?" She shook her head firmly while with her other hand seemed to shoo him away. I held my breath a moment to see if he would reach in anyway, but as if nothing were awry, he turned to unpack the bag he'd brought from home—Chinese rice bowls swaddled in bubblewrap, utensils bound in a rubber band. Sit there, he nodded at me, indicating the place opposite Deborah, meeting my gaze for an extra second with the same sun-speckled hazel eyes his mother had, and mouthing that everything was okay. Steam rose from the cartons as he opened them.

By the time he called her name again, he didn't seem fazed that she was still looking down, running her fingers over the string of pearls. But I felt my own breath tighten. Suppose she was worse off than he'd said. Suppose he hadn't told me the whole truth?

"Mom," he called yet again, walking over this time and laying his hand on her shoulder. "Soup?"

She looked up quickly. "Of course," she said, tucking her hand in her lap. "And some for Becca, too," she said smiling. "Becca, the dancer. Isn't that right? Mark tells me you're a marvelous dancer. Did he tell you how his father and I loved to dance?"

It would have been hard to hide the grin that came over Mark's face, or mine, as he ladled out the soup.

But I was only a beginner, I was quick to tell her. (So she wasn't a totterer after all!) It was her son who was the dance wizard. Without him, I might never have known how much I loved to

157

dance. Imagine! If I'd never gotten divorced, I would never have learned to dance. I would have missed dancing! But I didn't tell her these last thoughts about my other life, especially as I watched her face light up about Mark. "You mean the magician?" she said, going poof with her hands.

"Now, Madame," he said playfully. "Don't give away my secrets." He put a bowl of soup and a spoon in front of her then touched her cheek.

"Thank you for coming, Mark," she said quietly. She put her hand over his and patted his fingers. I could see where she'd worn her wedding rings, her finger an hourglass of bone.

"Shall we eat?" Mark asked, smiling and doing a little spin as he came back to his seat between me and his mother, not waiting before he sat down to start talking about our trip to the mountains. To the same cabin they went to. Did she remember? He didn't wait for her answer. He rambled on, recalling how the snow stacked on the trees, how the sunlight glistened. "Like diamonds," he said grinning, as if he fully expected her to nod in agreement. And the snow angels! Eat, he mouthed toward me, not pulling out the photo, but picking up his porcelain spoon and clinking it lightly on the table.

He must have noticed Deborah's eyes glazing over and then how she looked down into her lap, groping for something, her hands more and more frantic. When he looked down, too, I felt my own panic.

"Mark—?" she said, her voice strained and trembling. What was wrong? I waited for him to get up, rush to her side. But he didn't move. He kept his head down, his spoon tight in his fingers, his breath held, it seemed. Or was it just my breath?

"Mark," Deborah said, her voice quiet and taut. "Do you have my napkin?"

Mark looked up, his face pinched. "Of course, Mom," he said softly. He gestured toward the pile of paper napkins near me. That's all she wanted—a napkin?

Such a simple request. I handed her one, happy to help out. She took it and smiled. I waited for her to open it on her lap and sit back. We would eat now while Mark told more stories about the White Mountains.

But Mark didn't start speaking. The corners of his mouth grew tight as Deborah fumbled in her lap, unsnapped her purse, took out a pile of paper napkins all folded together, set the pile next to her bowl, and began, with her thumb and index finger, like someone peeling back skin, to unfold each fold and press open each crease. When the whole pile lay flat, she put the new napkin on top and began folding again. Perfect little triangles, one crease after another, until the pile was small enough for her to hold in her hand, to put it back in her purse. I waited to hear her open and close it, for the invitation to eat again. But as carefully as she made the pile, she began to unmake it, unfolding and flattening, adjusting each napkin until it was perfectly square with the others. Mark kept his face down.

I'm sorry, I wanted to whisper, to reach out to him.

But he didn't look up, not until she'd folded the napkins one more time and tucked them in her lap. "Mark," she said looking up, her eyes unusually bright. I could almost feel him take in a breath. "Did you ride the elevator?" She picked up her spoon and dipped it into her soup, smiling as if to herself. "Of course, any self-respecting fish explodes upon impact, right?" she said, then took her first spoonful of soup.

As Mark pushed back his chair to stand up, I started to get up, too. I would help him hail someone. We could take care of her. But he shook his head no. Stay, he mouthed as he walked over to Deborah and leaned down so his cheek nearly touched hers. "Is the soup good, Mom?" he asked quietly.

She nodded and smiled. "After this, we have chicken with cashews, right? And then fortunes, right?" She grinned as if getting her cues from the air. "Just what the doctor ordered. Right?"

Mark nodded and smiled, though I could see the sadness in his eyes.

"Well, then what are you waiting for?" she asked, gesturing toward his chair, his bowl. "We don't have all day."

For the rest of lunch, Mark told stories about the mountains, the snow that looked like whipped cream on the trees, the surprise of the hut keeper to see his mother. He told about his mother and father dancing, too, in their kitchen. Would his mother like to dance again? He could dance with her right now if she wanted. Or maybe on his birthday. Could they have a birthday dance? Promise? Deborah laughed as he talked, her face full of warmth and delight. All the while, the other residents pressed their noses to the windows and waved at us. How lovely to be feted like Mark's mom. We all waved back.

After the hour was up, Mark escorted his mother to her bedroom. When he came back, his lips taut, he took my hand and guided me through the maze of hallways. At each door, before he punched the exit code, he pointed to the flashing red lights and signage on the silver bars. *Please don't touch.*

"Terrible, isn't it," he whispered as we got outside, the words tight in his throat.

As I nodded in agreement, I wondered what it must feel like to lose your memory. Do you even know you're losing it, or is the brain kind in that way, disabling the very signals that tell you something is lost?

After we got down from the mountains, of course we went to the emergency room where they warmed my fingers the right way and told me not to break the bloody blisters, not to be scared by the bluish tinge of my flesh, and not to ignore the aching pain, because there were pain killers for that. As to what would happen next? They said they couldn't know for sure. Mark kept apologizing. He was so sorry.

He was also sorry because for the next two weeks, he had to be gone on business, a tech job in San Francisco. While he was away, I cleaned out my files, put in my hours at the gallery, and watched my third and fourth fingertips on my right hand turn black. Sometimes, when I could stomach it, I lay my fingers on the table and tried to pretend I didn't have two tips. Tried to pretend it didn't matter. Tried to pretend I wouldn't have to spend the rest of my life looking at those stubby fingers and remembering this mistake, too.

Now only time would tell. Would the tips shrivel up and fall off in a few months, or would the doctor decide it was smarter to make a clean cut?

Twice a day Mark called me. How was I? What could he do? He was so sorry. He loved me. Had anything changed? I'm sure he was referring to my fingers. But I couldn't bring myself to tell him about their blackness. I kept quiet out of kindness, I wanted to believe.

But I know it's not kindness I feel when the nurse, after my appointment, tells me Mark called to say his plane was delayed, and he's on his way to meet me at our favorite cafe. I shake my head, still shocked by the ease of the doctor's words. *Only two fingertips. You'll get accustomed to the loss.*

Mark is full of apology in the cafe. His plane circled O'Hare a million times. Nothing he could do about that. Or the missed connection. "But now tell me how you are," he says after he holds

162

me close. He sits down, pushing his jacket over the chair back, setting a bag on the floor, then leaning close as he reaches out and puts his hand, palm up, on the table, wiggling his fingers in invitation. "C'mon, Becca," he says, tapping his knuckles lightly.

If only I could reach out and take his hand. An hour ago, maybe, though even then, when the doctor asked to see my blackened fingers, I felt myself recoiling. "You got the frostbite where?" the doctor asked. "You got this how?"

Outside, people huddle at the bus stop, their backs turned to the wind, the snow banks their only buffer. The blizzard hit Philadelphia, too, along with the unrelenting bitter cold. Behind me, the door opens. People stomp their feet, clap their mittens. As a rush of cold air cuts across my neck, I push my hand deeper into my coat pocket, curl my fingers as if I could warm them, or feel them. I think about the other things I could have told the doctor. That the trip was Mark's idea, that he promised to keep me safe, that I trusted him. Or that Mark's flight came in long before he called me.

"I mean it, Becca," Mark says more urgently. "Give me your hand."

I shake my head.

Mark leans forward. "Listen, Becca." The anger in his voice surprises me. "As you know, my flight to Chicago was delayed and so I missed my connection. Not a damn thing I could do about—"

"You could have come directly from the airport," I say, my anger flaring to meet his. "You knew about the appoint—"

"But I didn't know how long—"

"But you did," I snap, my heart racing in that dangerous way anger has of making people feel alive.

He opens his mouth to speak. But just as quickly, he closes it, grabbing one of the napkins.

For a moment, I say nothing. I try to let my anger pass through me like the wind through the storefront sashes. My heart beats fast. So much I've planned to say to him. Like didn't he say he'd keep me safe? Didn't he promise? The questions mount in my mind, begging for their chance to come out on the table. Anything to save myself from having to look at my blackened fingers and remember—but forever!—how I forgot to take care of myself.

I take a big breath to begin. "When you first invited me—"

"Becca, shush," he says, his voice low in his throat. For a second, he bores his eyes into mine. "Why don't you begin by telling me where you were a half hour ago." He pauses. Takes a breath. "Like where you were when I called you—okay, from my mother's."

I sit very still. His mother's?

"Why didn't you pick up, Becca?" he presses on, thrumming the table as if he were waiting, but not waiting my answer. "You knew I would call, Becca," he says more insistently. "You probably

164

even heard me on the message machine. Why didn't you pick up?"

For a moment, I hold my breath. In my mind, I see the picture I haven't planned to pass along. The phone ringing. Myself standing next to it. Not wanting to pick up the receiver. Not wanting to touch anything. Not wanting anything to touch me.

"Becca," Mark says, his voice softer now. "I love you."

I shake my head. He went to see his mother? "You think if you say those words, everything is—"

"Look. I brought you a present."

"Mark, I'm trying to say something."

"A gift," he says, reaching into the brown bag next to him.

"You're not listening," I say. "You think everything about our trip is—"

"Did I tell you it was my birthday?" he asks, pulling out a shoebox wrapped in beautiful blue paper.

I pause.

"And on my birthday," he speaks a little faster, "I can give you a gift or tell you I love you as much as I want. A million times, if I feel like it." He hesitates a second. "Even if it weren't my birthday." He pushes the box closer.

"Well, is it?"

"I had to go see her first," he starts to explain.

I shake my head, caught between wonder and disbelief. I'm losing my fingers and he had to go see his mother? To keep a

165

promise for someone who won't remember his birthday anymore than she might remember—?

For a moment my anger is gone, or maybe pushed so deep, it feels like sadness. "Happy Birthday," I say softly. "But now let me speak."

"But why?" He leans forward, his sharp whisper seeming to come up out of nowhere, cutting into the air, startling me with his challenge. "So you can keep blaming me for the storm? Or for the canister I simply forgot to fill—a human error? Or for the people who locked up Gray Knob without my knowing? Or for every goddamn hurt buried in your heart? Becca, c'mon now. I love you," he says, his voice grown raspy with intensity.

"You didn't tell me you loved me, before," I say, trying to keep my voice firm.

Mark tilts his head and stares at me. "But I do."

"No." My voice is shaking. "You think saying that makes everything okay."

Mark takes a deep breath. He folds his hands in front of him on the table. All those fingers neatly meshed.

"And suppose I really love you," he says quietly.

"Suppose you just want someone to love you back."

"Suppose there's nothing wrong with that?"

"Suppose you just want a good follower?"

"Suppose you're being goddamn ridiculous!" He hits the table with his fingers.

"Then try this on for size," I say, taking out my hand and laying it just where he wants it. Under his very eyes. Let him take in the shock of my blackened fingers.

I expect him to wince, which he does. But I don't expect him—or maybe I do—to cup his hands and take mine gently in his. To hold it. To blow warm air on the thick black line across the two tips. So easy to see where the gangrene stops. Like a sign. Cut here.

"The doctor said I'd get used to the loss," I say, the sarcasm rising on its own. "He said—" but here my voice shuts down. I can barely whisper the rest. "'In time, I won't notice the difference.'"

Mark sits perfectly still, staring at my fingers. With his thumb, he begins to circle the hollow of my palm, pressing on my life lines. Then he reaches to touch the blackness. Instinctively, I pull back.

"I'm sorry," he says, looking right at me. "Does it hurt?"

All along I've planned to say yes. All the way up my wrist, my arm, my neck. All night. All day. To make him feel my pain. My numbness. My loss. But as I take a breath to speak, nausea overcomes me. The nausea of the body talking, emptying itself of a fear it doesn't need anymore.

"Tell me the truth, Becca," he says, slowly. "Does it hurt? Does something hurt?"

The words are slow in coming. "No," I whisper. "Right now it only throbs."

Flower Sunday

Andrew, it's time for church," Celia calls out to the patio. She hovers for a moment in the doorway, watching him turn the pages of the *San Francisco Chronicle*. She knows he doesn't care about Flower Sunday, the last day of church before summer vacation, the day everyone gets a flower to take home and plant. But she wishes he'd get up cheerfully anyway, as if he were as eager as she to see their friends at church, to talk with them. Sometimes she thinks about going alone. She wouldn't have to bother him that way. Wouldn't have to be the nag. But then she'd be by herself. What would people think? What would she think?

She waits a moment for him to stir. When he keeps reading, she goes out to help him. Not that he needs her help. He's a little achy in his hips, just as she is—both of them in their sixties—but otherwise he's perfectly able to do whatever he wants. Maybe that's what bothers her.

"Andrew," she says, trying to sound cheerful as she stands

next to his chair and reminds him it's time to go. Behind him, a curtain of roses tumbles from the lattice fence. Thirty years ago, when they entered this second marriage for both of them, they planted these roses. Little bushes then. She wonders if he's noticed the profusion of scarlet blossoms today, how full they are this year. The rain has done that.

She's glad when without further prompting he sets the newspaper down on the patio and pushes himself up from the chaise lounge. As he follows her into the bedroom, she chats about the friends they'll see and how she'll miss them over the summer. Won't he? When he doesn't answer, she keeps babbling. She's going to wear her light blue chiffon dress with the white sweeps of willow on it. Will he wear the blue tie she gave him last fall for his sixty-eighth birthday? Blue to match his eyes. She still loves his eyes.

"Mmmmm," he says, taking his summer suit from the closet and humming a little as he puts it on then cinches the blue tie around his neck.

For a moment she almost thinks to ask him how he feels about this entry into summer—this time when people go their separate ways. Like traveling capsules, she muses, wondering if he's noticed how much they, too, seem to go their own separate ways, not outside the house, but inside. But it all seems to work, doesn't it? she thinks, standing in front of the mirror as she reaches over her head to grab her dress zipper, her bony elbow sticking up like a protruding root. She can't help but notice the bags under her eyes, the skin sagging under her chin. Does Andrew notice these signs of aging? Or does he focus instead on the softness of her skin, the meals she cooks, the way she makes their bed each morning, folding the coverlet so it tucks perfectly over the pillows?

"I do so much like Flower Sunday," she says, as if he'd just asked her her feelings.

"Mmmmm," he murmurs, padding into the bathroom.

As always, Celia waits for him by the front door. In the mirror, she notices she's forgotten her lipstick. She undoes the pearl button tab on her little white satin purse—it used to be her mother's—takes out her red gloss, and glides it over her lips, pressing them together like she and they share a secret. When she puts the gloss back in her bag, she thinks how she loves having a purse that opens and closes without a sound. She tucks the bag under her arm, knowing Andrew will emerge in his own sweet time, the usual water spots on his pants, his cuffs flopping around his brown-tooled shoes. Like always, he'll hold the door open for her, lock it behind them, then follow her down the front walkway, past the gardenias and pock-marked oranges to the avocado tree, where she'll wait so they can cross the street together, her hand set in the crook of his arm. Sometimes when they cross, she thinks about what a ballroom dance teacher once said eons ago. "The woman is the truck, the man the truck driver." She shakes her head. Imagine her, a truck!

At church, after Reverend Macon sermonizes about the bounty of summer, Celia chats with friends while Andrew stands at her side. Fred Dappleby, the old golf pro, tells them the boys are going down to the Pebble Beach Classic without the girls this time. Does Andrew want to come? he asks, winking at Celia. She can't help remarking to herself how changed Fred seems since Esther's death in April. Rumor has it he and his new housekeeper have something going, a fact Celia finds repugnant. Hettie Bastion waxes eloquent about the clusters of peonies her husband Sam helped her divide and replant last fall. "They've never done better," Hettie boasts as Sam takes her hand. Sam cautions Andrew to sell their Taurus and get a new car while they can still come out ahead.

On their walk home, gazing at the shiny white magnolia blossoms, Celia thinks about Sam's advice. It's been months since she asked Andrew about selling the old car. She really wants a new one. What does Andrew think now about Sam's idea, she asks. There's a familiar huff in his voice as he reminds her Sam is big on quick trades.

"You and I have always driven our cars into the ground, Celia. Why change now?" he says, cupping his yellow zinnia in his hand, bobbing it like he's trying to figure out how much it weighs.

Because I want a new car, Celia is tempted to say, but she knows her answer will only annoy him. And annoyance isn't good for either of them, she reminds herself, looking down at her orange pansy with a violet center, recalling the doctor's advice at her last check-up. Think positively. It will be good for both of you.

"Didn't we have a nice time, though!" she says, quickening her step as they turn onto their street. She starts to chat about the people they saw, being careful to say nothing about Fred's housekeeper or his wife's death. Or about Sam and Hettie holding hands. She pretends everything is fine—and it will be—as Andrew unlocks the door and pushes it open for her. "Voilà!" He hands her his flower as he enters—so she can plant it by the front door, as she always does—and beelines in front of her for the bedroom. Celia knows exactly what's on his mind. Sunday noon. The Palo Alto sun streaking onto the patio to heat up his bones.

Without a word, he changes into his khaki shorts and plaid short-sleeved shirt, casting his other shirt onto the pile Celia will take to the cleaners on Monday. Celia changes, too, but faster, so she's already in the kitchen when he passes through to the warm terrace, church a mere blip on his screen. When the patio door jumps its track as he opens it, he yanks it back. "Ah," she hears him sigh as he settles onto his chaise lounge. As he lifts the newspaper onto his lap, Celia can almost feel how warm and crinkly it is against his skin. She can wait until after lunch, she decides, to ask again about a new car. She doesn't want to be pushy, but she really would like something new. After all, it is she who drives them everywhere these days. Andrew tends to nod off at the wheel. She swears he almost killed her last year turning left into oncoming traffic. How could he have not seen the car? She still gets heated when she talks about it to her grown children on the phone.

"Why, I had a concussion for weeks after that."

"Mother, why don't you leave him if you're so unhappy?" her youngest daughter said the last time they talked.

Tears come into Celia's eyes when she thinks about this conversation. Her children still don't understand how hard it was to be widowed, raising four children by herself.

"I would be so alone," she whispered.

"Think of it as being by yourself. There's a difference," her daughter said.

For me, it would be alone. Celia hears again these words echo in her head as she takes a new can of beef consommé from the fridge, clamps it onto the electric opener, and watches it spin, the scalloped edge opening like a Venus flytrap. She takes out the usual fluted porcelain bowl and tilts the can over it. With a slosh, the jellied soup suctions loose. She tops the shiny mass with a dollop of sour cream. Just one bowl today, she decides. She'll make something different for herself. Later.

"Here's lunch," she says, yanking open the screen door, knowing everything will be fine after they eat. Out in the sun, she stands for a moment and studies Andrew behind the newspaper. She wonders if he would laugh to see how his fingers, legs, and floppy feet protrude like cutouts around the Neiman Marcus

174

ladies on the back page strutting in their strapless dresses. They're in vogue again, Celia says to herself, sighing as she puts down the bowl and spoon, remembering how she used to wear those dresses herself.

But of course things change as you get older, she says to herself, gazing at the scarlet roses that tumble over the lattice fence. For a moment she thinks back to the day they tore up the old flower beds and decided which roses to plant. She wanted the large-flowering Don Juans. "Deep velvet scarlet. Classic high-centered form. Very fragrant. Vigorous," she read right from the book, chuckling at the description. But Andrew said he'd rather not. He'd smelled them at the nursery—too strong. And too pointy. Would she mind this other—Paul's Scarlet Climber—which grew in clusters of red flounces? "Like petticoats," he'd said, smiling.

"Even if they 'tend to turn unpleasantly purple when old'?" she remembers reading straight from the book. "Even if they 'sweep less'?" But just last week, after all these years, she discovered she'd said the wrong thing. Leafing through the tattered guide, she'd paused at the dog-eared page and seen not "sweep less" but "weep less." That's what she should have said to Andrew way back then. "Do you still want them even if they weep less?" Instead she'd asked if he minded that the cool nights would keep the fragrance at bay?

"All the better," he'd replied.

So, Paul's Scarlet Climber it was. And not so terrible, after all, Celia thinks, gazing at the blossoms bowing down with their own weight. Sometimes, when nobody's around, she strokes them. Ever so lightly because she knows, as the season goes on, they fall at the merest touch if you press too hard, leaving the roses denuded, exposing everything. On some days she puts her face close to them and admires their rich colors, their yellow stamens feathered like moths' antennae. She breathes in their sweetness. Blood-rich breath to her.

But the roses are starting to turn purple. Time to cut them back. She looks down at her hands and flexes them. She can still easily stretch an octave on the piano. Flowers are just flowers, she thinks to herself. They'll come back next year. They always have. But still she feels sad.

"The roses have been so full this year," she says, thinking Andrew might hear her sadness, might comfort her.

Nothing.

"And the grass," she says, noticing how it's taking over the garden. "Do you see how it's grown?" She walks to the garden's edge.

Still nothing.

She sighs. She loves her garden, she says to herself, knowing she'll weed it on her own today. Like always. *Buck up*, her mother's words come back to her in a whisper as she kneels on the yellow vinyl pad Andrew gave her for Christmas last year, pulls her trowel from the dirt, and eyes the crab grass slowly engulfing the irises. She plunges her trowel into the closest bunch of grass. The yellow tongues on the irises quiver. She jabs again.

"What I hate"—she says, deciding she'll just talk with herself, then—"is how the garden"—she takes hold of the grass and yanks—"loses its"—the clump pulls free—"shape!" This last word comes out as a small explosion, rocking her back. Flecks of dirt fly into her face. She spits them out then drops the clump at the garden's edge, cuts at it with her trowel, knocking away the encrusted dirt before she pitches it up and down. She has to admit she loves how the clump gets lighter as the dirt falls back into the hole where it belongs, the roots shaking loose. She flings the remains onto the weed pile in the corner, looking over her shoulder for a second. Andrew is pattering his fingers on the edge of the business section, scanning the lists of commodities, no doubt, running figures through his brain. A retired math professor, he takes pleasure in computing things, watching over their retirement, he insists. After all those years of being in an office. His pleasure, now.

Celia puts the trowel down a moment, thinking about his request. Surely she can grant him this time, this space, now. She rests her hands on her thighs and gazes out to the field beyond the barbed wire fence along the back of their property, where mottled eucalyptus trees, the bark fraying on their twisted limbs, stand in a little grove. Next to them, olive trees flash silver in the sunlight.

She and Andrew have always found the trees beautiful. Today is no different. She stares at them, tracing the grass that licks at their trunks, then runs like wildfire under the garden fence.

"Sometimes I feel like the back lot is *invading*," she says, thinking about his pleasure—and hers. She's a little surprised at just how much she really does want Andrew to look at her, to pay attention. Which he does. Is someone coming? he wants to know. He looks toward the front walk. When he sees no one, he smiles at her before retreating behind the paper again. But he's smelled the soup. Or maybe he's seen it.

"Mmmmm," he says, leaning over to take a spoonful. He pulls the jellied mass through his teeth then tucks behind the paper again.

But Celia knows she can get his attention now. Food does that for him. "Andrew," she says, standing up and walking over. "Could you do me a favor?" She's a little surprised at herself—making such an obvious demand.

"I can't right now," he says from behind the newsprint.

"But Andrew," she says, stepping to block his sun. She feels a surge in her body, like an engine revving. "Could you just get the stepladder from the kitchen for me? I need it to cut the roses."

"Celia," he says, letting go with one of his hands and waving it as if to shoo her away. "You can leave the flowers. They'll be fine on their—"

"No, they won't," Celia says so quickly her sharpness

178

surprises her. She leans over the paper and draws her face close to his. "For your information, flowers need cutting back. They grow better if you do that. Like Hettie's peonies," she adds at the last second, though of course she knows—you don't cut peonies back. You divide them. As if Andrew knows the difference.

"Celia—" he says. "It's Sunday—"

"Never mind," she snaps, suddenly tired of all of it. She glares at him a second then turns about-face and walks to the garage to get the long-nosed clippers. They're the wrong kind for delicate work, but she doesn't care. She'll manage with whatever, she says to herself as she returns to the patio to find Andrew with the newspaper folded on his lap, his hands held out to her. She shakes her head. Too late now. You missed your chance, she wants to say to him as she sets the clippers down on the stones and turns without a word to get the stepladder. When the screen door sticks and jumps its track, she doesn't even call back to him, *why don't you at least fix the damn door*, though she's tempted. But she's already marching on her own, back to the garden, right by him and the newspaper he's reading again. She plants the ladder under the sweep of roses, pushes the legs securely into the dirt, gets her clippers, and climbs the three rubberized steps. A thorned cane catches her shirt as she ascends. She pries it away then eyes the nearest cluster, stretching out the handles of the clippers and thrusting them inward. They close with a tidy snap. The branch drops like a dead weight.

Celia moves to the next branch. Snip. The space suddenly

179

opens up. She feels a quiver of excitement, sees the next offenders, and reaches a little bit farther. Snip. Snip. Celia likes the sound of the hardened metal rasping against itself. She likes the feel of her arms, open, closed, snip, snip, muscles taut, carving out this space before her very eyes.

Soon she's no longer appraising the bushes carefully, but moving the ladder wherever and cutting more blindly, more wildly, enjoying the feeling she imagines a sharpshooter must have at a practice range. With each hit maybe he feels, as she does, that something unexpected is released, that scores are balanced: this one for the beef consommé—lop—this one for his falling asleep at the table—snip—this one for the dirty clothes he expects her to wash—gone—for the endless lists and dinners and thank you notes, and this one, yes, for the affection—she snips hard—the affection not returned—a big branch that falls with difficulty because it has so many offshoots she has to disentangle it from the fence and push it to the ground, where scarlet petals lie everywhere. For a moment, she wants to take off her shoes and walk on the velvet carpet, feel the satin between her toes. But there are thorns on the branches, too.

She stops cutting. Sweat drips down her brow. Mosquito welts rise on her arms.

"I'm done," she announces, hearing the mixture of triumph and fatigue in her voice.

"Mmmmm," Andrew says from behind the newsprint.

Flower Sunday

"No, I'm done," she says again with a greater tone of finality, determined this time to get his attention. A job well done. As she comes down the ladder, the newspaper rustles. Andrew peers out from behind it.

"That's nice," he says, glancing up toward the flowers.

But it's not nice. Celia has turned to look at the roses. Jagged points stick up everywhere. The skirts and flounces are all gone. Even the ones that would have lasted another week. Oh my, she thinks. Oh my.

But without a word, she takes the clippers back to the garage and returns for the stepladder, wondering if he will say something. Does he notice how terrible it looks? Will he commiserate?

"Celia," he says as she passes by. She pauses as he reaches out his hand. "The wetness from the rains is seeping through this damn chair cushion," he says, gesturing toward it, where the foam squishes underneath him. "Would you mind bringing out a towel when you come back?"

"But I'm not coming back," she says, for a second letting herself wonder—if she kept on walking right through the front door instead of going in to lie down, what would he say?

Andrew's eyes widen.

"Just what do you want?" he asks, his voice chafing.

She stands still. Her neck aches. Her arms throb from all that cutting. Your help, she could tell him. That's all. But even this isn't the truth, she realizes. She wants something much simpler, something so simple she feels foolish at the thought of having to tell him. She wants him to watch her, to praise her, to share her sadness, to hold her hand.

But how preposterous, she tries to comfort herself as she yanks open the screen door one more time. To imagine after all these years that he would do that. What was she thinking? Without another word, she goes to lie down on her side of the bed, rests her hand palm up on her forehead, feels her blood pounding. She must calm herself. Quell this momentary anger.

She will think about her roses. Will remember them as they were before, and as they will be again. Paul's Scarlet Climber. She takes a deep breath. What would Andrew say if he knew their other name? *Danse du feu.* Or if he knew, in roses, the male organs also give off the fragrance? "Weren't you kind of banishing yourself not wanting the fragrance?" she might have asked him years ago. But it's too late, now. She should have paid attention back then. Now he would only look at her and puzzle. What on earth was she talking about?

About her roses. About herself. About how she loves that roses are male and female in one flower, that the ladies' skirts conceal everything, that the pistil is the female part. How she loves that word. *Pistil. Pistil. Pistil.* She chants it loud and louder to herself until the hiss and the whistle that comes between her lips tickles her mouth and for a moment makes her laugh—and cry silently— at her own folly.

Point of Distraction

The first thing Cindy does when she arrives at the island house is unscrew the dining room table legs and put them in the fireplace. Then she carries the table top down to the beach and throws it in the water. "Why isn't the kitchen table adequate?" she will say to Rob when he comes out on the noon boat. "Why so much stuff?"

"Could you at least tell me what prompted this rash move?" he asks when he arrives four hours later. He stands in the middle of the big open room, the kitchen at one end, the living and dining areas at the other, and runs his fingers through his thinning hair. He can hardly believe his eyes. The nested wooden coffee tables, the walnut ones, lie in pieces in the fireplace, the flames licking around them. ("Go ahead, get them out," she says, but he can see they're already charred.) The thin wine glasses with the extra long stems lie splintered in the trash. "Where's the china?" he asks with growing alarm. He sees the cupboard doors open, the space where the blue-rimmed plates belong, plates bought when they got married fifteen years ago because she loved the color. A second marriage for both of them. Cindy points out the big windows, down to the water. He can see the damask sofa cushions, the green ones from the couch, bobbing in the receding tide. All six of them. Surely ruined by now.

"But I don't see the china," he says, trying hard to keep a calm voice, as if he were merely unable to see a star or a blue heron or a mottled sand crab hiding under the rocks.

"Of course you can't," Cindy says softly to reassure him. "It's hard to see the pieces. But when the sun glints just right, you can see the shards there by the water's edge. Here, come this way a little." She uses her outstretched arm to sight, as if it were a rifle. She did that for real a few times once. Target practice. Clay pigeons. She was pretty good.

"I was thinking how much the island children, in a few years, will love to find the small pieces in the next cove over," she says enthusiastically. "You know, where the sea glass always washes up after the storms? The children will be charmed to find the signature pieces. Can you imagine that?"

What is she talking about, imagining *anything* in the wake of such destruction? Rob can hardly speak as he looks around. The glass coffee table, the old maple rocker, the extra dining room chairs, the posters from the walls, the collection of conch shells

184

(all the way from Antigua!)—where are they? It doesn't make sense. When he arrived, coming up the rickety gangplank, him against gravity, there she was, waving as always with the dog leash in her hand. She even kissed him hello, right on the lips.

"Hey, where's Buckley?" He's almost afraid to ask.

Cindy walks into the middle of the room, wide open now, and thinks this over. Buckley. Yes, where did she see him last? He was with her when she went to meet the boat. She saw him spraying at the Alcott's laundry line post, the McVeigh's garbage can, the mail house steps, the pilings. How she tired of waiting while he lifted his leg at every turn. These male dogs. Such oddities. Spraying like old lady perfume bottles. She chuckles at the image. Buckley raising his leg just so, spritzing everywhere. Such a male compulsion, this one, to mark territory.

"But why are you laughing?" Rob tilts his head, squints one eye, and scrutinizes her as if he can tell something by the dilation of her pupils. He's an optometrist. He looks at his watch. She knows what he's thinking. Low tide in two hours.

"I'm sure Buckley's around here somewhere," she says, full of confidence. But where? She walks back in her mind. First to the marsh. She remembers seeing him trot into the reeds, his black head held high. She almost followed him, eager to see what lured him—was it the baby ducks?—but she went back into the house instead to finish her last chore. To run a cloth over the sills where the line of trinkets used to be—snail shells converted into little animals, old-fashioned candy dishes filled with thumbtacks and paper clips, coasters with antique sailboats on them (a present from her ex-father-in-law). Such a pain to dust around those little knickknacks—but now it would be easy. One clean sweep.

But had she dusted, after all? She eyes the sill under the huge picture window, sees the pattern of each disappeared thing, silhouetted squares and rounds. Surely Rob will notice the empty circles. He might even go down to the beach right now to look for the things that would float—and then what? Will everything come uncovered as the tide goes out?

Oh my, Cindy thinks. With the blender and the beater, the bread maker and the nuker, she'd known better, been smarter, gone to the far point, climbed over the jagged rocks and bubbly seaweed that popped underfoot, and thrown them into deeper water. She was thinking then. Thinking with pleasure about using a simple whisk, about kneading bread with the weight of her own body. Whatever happened to using our hands? She looks down at hers, pausing only a moment to take in the little cuts on her fingertips. But they won't hold her back, she thinks with relief, looking up to scan the empty Formica kitchen counter. Rest your eyes on me, it says. I am free now, like the wide channel in front of your house, unbroken by wind or current.

But Rob isn't looking at the counter. He's staring out the window. Cindy follows his gaze, only hers goes farther, across the channel dotted with lobster buoys to where the old stone fort bulges out from the back of House Island. Or is it the front? How do you know on an island what is front or back?

Cindy smiles reassuringly to herself. On this island, it's obvious. The houses are on the front. It has to be called the front, because that's where the people are. On the back are trails and a camouflaged fort, overgrown with green spindly vines so thick you don't know where the fort is anymore, except for the gun turrets and towers. Those you can climb and look out toward Portugal, if you want (there is one small slice of rocky island first), or toward Portland and Mt. Washington, which this morning she'd been able to see from the beach, a cap of snow on the mountain top, it had been that clear and cold. Which is why her fingers hurt after throwing all those things in the icy water, retrieving the ones that didn't go far enough and throwing them again. Even the broken china. Salt stung the cuts on her fingertips from all that throwing. If she'd put on Band-Aids, Rob might have thought she was hiding something.

"Cindy," he says. He walks out the door onto the deck, signals for her to follow. He leans against the railing, the water sparkling behind him. He needs to ask her if her friend Clara is behind all this, which is the only reason he can stay calm for now. (Cindy can't have gone crazy, can she?) "Did Clara die?" he asks in a gentle whisper. Or is it Lauren—not officially his step-daughter because he came along too late for that, but still he cares for her. "Did something happen to Lauren?"

187

Cindy shakes her head, looks down at her feet. They're warm, now, she thinks.

"Then what possessed you?" Rob nearly pleads.

She looks into his worried face, his hazel-flecked eyes deep and unflinching. This man she loves. She feels the sudden urge to smile at him, joke with him. Possessed. Possessions. Did he use that word on purpose? A burst of exhilaration races through her as she thinks back to how it felt to throw things off the rocks. How she almost hadn't been able to scamper fast enough for her giddiness. The sense of lightness from tossing all those things over the edge, though she'd saved his old toaster. Did he notice it next to the honey in the cupboard?

What can she tell him, she wonders, to put his heart at ease?

My feet are warm now, she might say. Even by the time you arrived, they'd recovered from that brutal water. It was so cold, Rob, sharp like ice.

But he will want to know more, will want answers. Answers she actually tried to figure out on her and Buckley's standard three-mile hike around the island this morning. First to the eastern tower that looked out over the rest of Maine, to where the trawlers churned up the channel and the buoys sucked hard with the tide. Then along the back, where Buckley chased deer, their stubby white tails flicked in sudden erections as they dashed into the underbrush and he plunged in after them. Then down the long gradual hill to the Point, where a stone gazebo looked out to the rocks that jabbed like outstretched fingers into the sea. Stupid Buckley thought he might catch the cormorants sitting on the fingertips, hanging out their wings like clothes on a line. Several times he slid down the slippery sides of the rocks, splashing through the tide pools and into the foaming surf, his blood driving him to do that. Every time Cindy called him back, but silly dog, he never listened. He splashed around, battered, until he decided he couldn't reach the birds. Holding his jaw just above the cresting water, he rose with the waves onto the small section of beach and shook himself before beginning anew. Every time Cindy worried. She knew how slippery the rocks were.

"I didn't know I was going to throw things in the water, Rob," she says. She would much rather tell him how glad she was when Buckley headed into the underbrush again, out of the treacherous surf, because then she was free to sit and think. But she knows she needs to give Rob answers. What possessed her to throw all that stuff in the ocean? What will he believe?

She walks to the railing as she ponders, eager to stand close to him. Suppose she tells him the things that went through her mind. Wouldn't the house rise like Noah's ark when the animals got off? Or would it be like Archimedes? Yes, her heart starts to race again. Archimedes when he stepped out of the bathtub and suddenly there was less water. Less weight. Less displacement. It's very straightforward, her reasons for throwing things into the sea, she'd have to say. For what does the sea care, whose level changes daily and unceasingly. The sea knows how to manage all that weight, Cindy is sure of it. Sometimes she fills a bucket with water and lifts it up to imagine being the sea. Or she fills a bucket with sand and thinks about how the earth manages all that weight, too.

"I think it was the rocks that made me do it," she says to Rob, not at all sure this is true or right. But she *did* sit on the rocks this morning, like other mornings, and rub her feet into hollows as smooth and worn as monument steps, admiring what the waves can do. Here a gentle satin seat, while on the rock next door, coarse wormy holes and cracks that scraped her fingers and cut them when she ran her hand back and forth. She was careful as she made her way along these rocks, wondering all the while what people would say when they heard what she did. Was that Rob's biggest worry?

She imagines the islanders' voices. Their gossip down by Mermaid Rock on Big Beach, where the island children once took old house paint to create a supine sea lady, full-breasted, her hair like seaweed twirling down to her tail fins. Cindy must be lonely, they'll say. Her only child—done with graduate school and far away, as yet unmarried. Too bad Cindy never had more children. Divorced too soon. Remarried too late. There must be emptiness now. Sorrow welling up.

But no. That isn't it at all. Lauren is leading her own life—

what mother wouldn't want that for her child? Of course, she worries about Lauren's ending up alone. It's hard to grow older and be alone. But heavens, Lauren still has so much of her life in front of her! As to more children? She and Rob didn't want more children in their first marriages, so why would they want them in their second? There was his work and her painting, now that she's painting again. There are nieces and nephews. And, of course, there are the island children.

But still the islanders will prattle, latching onto that stale notion about needing more children with the same tenacity Buckley latches onto a stick. As if only children matter.

Or is it lost love, they might whisper. Who? Her? Rob? Oh, both once had their momentary flights. But not now. No, Cindy doesn't feel unloved or unloving, for what after all is love but her early arrival at the dock, keen to see the boat on the horizon. Or the kiss she gave Rob when he arrived up the gangplank, squarely on his mouth, thinking how soft and gentle his lips are, how her heart quiets to know he's here.

Maybe they'll say it's depression or craziness, but to these voices, she can only laugh a little. (Wouldn't craziness be a relief, to throw everything to the wind like that?) Who isn't crazy who makes it through this life? She thinks of her list of sorrows. So much like everyone else's. A high school beau killed by a drunk driver. Suzanne raped by her uncle. Melanie falling out of a tree and breaking her neck. Matthew and Deborah's house burned.

Barbara, Peter, David, Margaret—the list goes on and on. We all suffer. And yet we live on. So what's the point of gossiping, she thinks as she gazes out to the water and recalls how she skirted the shoreline, careful not to walk on the rocks that cut her feet, but to stay on the smooth ones, to block out all those islanders' voices, nosy and incriminating. She thinks about how careful she was to curl her long toes over the smooth rocks, springing from one to the other, torquing her knees and ankles until she arrived at the small cove where thousands of small round boulders leaned naturally against each other.

"The rocks are lovely on the other side," she says to Rob, taking his hand, leading him inside, out of the wind.

"Cindy, what are you talking about?" he asks, but he lets his hand stay in hers as they stand by the big windows.

About the rocks in the cove, she thinks. The perfectly round, black and white speckled rocks. The oval rocks. Always harder to cut an oval, anyone knows that. Piles and piles of them, sparkling in the light. Some with rose quartz running down their middles. Some with mica that catches your eye like distraction.

"I went out to the Point this morning," she says. "But first, you're right, I dismantled the table."

"Cindy, you dismantled everything. Are you crazy? What will—"

"—people say?" She fills in quickly. "Is that what worries you?"

Rob sighs. No, he just threw that out. A subterfuge. He has bigger worries. Like loneliness. Is that coming back to haunt her? Or could it be their decision to move away from her hometown? But she was at peace with that. Does she have a lover? Would that ever happen again? But he can't imagine it. So maybe it *is* Clara, after all.

"Are you sure it's not Clara?" he asks hesitantly. When his mother died, he remembers how he couldn't speak at first.

Cindy stares at the wide channel. (Almost low tide. What will appear first?) She thinks about the quiet of the bowered woods, the sound of the lapping waves as they roll up the stony beach. Out in front of the house, a lone lobsterman is pulling up his traps, hand over hand. For a second she wonders: When objects move through the water, do they feel the weight of their own wake? Or is there a point where they all rise up? Like the boat this morning. Should she tell Rob about the boat? Would he understand?

"Cindy, what is it?" Rob asks, his voice quiet, insistent. He puts his hand on her shoulder to turn her to him.

"It must have been the sea smelts," she says softly. Her word, he knows, for when the sea smells so full and rich it covers you like a heavy cloak, or a salve, anointing every part of your body until you think you have to lie down or scoop it up in your hands and smear it all over the world. For comfort. For protection.

Rob nods and smiles. He's always liked this phrase of hers. It reminds him of the only smelts he knows. The buckets and buckets of real smelts, arched and silver in the moonlight of his childhood. Scooped from the streams, more in the mad rush than anyone could possibly eat.

"But it wasn't really the sea smelts this time," she says when she sees his face relax. How she loves to see him smile. "Not even the sea," she says, hearing her voice race a little, the words only crystallizing now. "It was this morning's boat. The way it rose high on its own crest and stayed there, all the way across the channel." She pauses as Rob tilts his head and squints. Dubious.

"I know what the island people will think," she tumbles ahead. "But suppose I just wanted us to be free like that, to rise up out of the water? Isn't that possible? Credible? Must there always be a real reason?"

"Well, isn't there?" he asks, searching her eyes.

What can she say to appease him? He needs something solid. Something he can hold in his hands, his mind. Maybe she should tell him, it's true. Clara's family called last night. Clara is in the hospital again with a high fever. Cindy is sure the word "dead" will come down the wire before she can figure out the right thing to say. Oh, it would make a tidy explanation. "A friend dying. It sent her off the deep end." But that's not it, Cindy is thinking. It isn't Clara, but the weight of everything piled up. All of life piled up. That's why she loves the rocks at the Point. Weighty but small. Smooth and warm. Carry me, they say. Hold me.

Recently Rob has been telling her to "be careful." So today, like every day, she heeded his words. She didn't go too close to the water's edge or stay in the freezing channel too long. She didn't slip off the cliff with the kitchen goods. She didn't run into the marsh or into the roiling surf. She wasn't late for the boat. And she didn't lose Buckley, because here he is, barking to be let in.

"There's no simple answer," she says, hoping Rob knows how much she heeds his words. "I just needed fewer things. More space. You know?" She likes how her voice fills the emptiness. Rob will like it too. He will understand. He of all people, who loves her.

But something has caught his eye in the receding tide. The old rocker hung up on the rocks.

"I need to bring it back," he says.

"Of course." She turns to him. "If it matters, get it."

He's already headed out the door, across the deck, and down the path to the beach. She follows behind him, stopping on the sand to watch as he walks with his clothes on up to his chest into the water. Holding his hands above his head, he makes his way over to the emerging boulders, lifts the rocker up high, turns, and walks back, pushing against the tide. At the water's edge, he sets the rocker down facing House Island. She comes and stands by him while he shivers and rocks, and together they watch the sea.

Acknowledgments

For their inspiration, encouragement, and examples of persistence and courage, I wish to thank my faculty colleagues and students in the brief-residency MFA in Writing Program at Spalding University. I also wish to thank Sena Jeter Naslund, whose vision and artistry have given me and countless others a journey through writing that reaches for the very highest.

For their care in reading, editing, and managing the publication of this collection, I also want to thank Adriena Dame, Kathleen Driskell, Kim Stinson-Hawn, Katy Yocom, and especially Karen Mann.

Thanks also to my writing friends, who over the years have shared their energy, wisdom, and support—Talvi Ansel, Andrea Hollander Budy, Peter Covino, Gigi Edwards, Sally Hartshorne, Bob Leuci, Selma Moss-Ward, Katherine and David Porter, Jo Porter, Jill Storey, Beth Taylor, Elizabeth Testa, Nicki Toler, and Bavari Su Ulz. Thanks also to editors Laurence Goldstein and Ben George for their generosity in suggesting valuable revision ideas before moving my work into print.

To Dianne Benedict, Wesley Brown, Jaimee Wriston Colbert, Abby Frucht, Doug Glover, David Jauss, Ellen Lesser, Chris Noel, Kathleen Spivack, Sharon Sheehe Stark, Julia Thacker, and A.J. Verdelle, thank you for sharing your gifts as teachers and writers.

I also wish to thank the Harvard Expository Writing Program

for some financial support, and my colleagues and students at Harvard, Brown, and the University of Rhode Island, for their enthusiasm and support. Thanks also to the master gardeners of Santa Clara County for their counsel.

Finally, thanks bigger than words to my family—to my dad, who died too long ago to know I would become a writer, to my mom and twin, both of whom would have loved to see this collection in print, and to Steve, Chieko, Lin, Peter, Emily, Tom, Kate, and Yin—who continue to share their courage, heart, and patience.

Last, to Mike, without whom I couldn't have done this, and to my incredible daughters, Jess and Herrick, thank you for enduring and believing in me, and for continuing to exhort and inspire me to tell the truth in my fiction.

About the Author

Jody Lisberger's prize-winning fiction has appeared in *Confrontation*, *Fugue*, *Michigan Quarterly Review*, *The Louisville Review*, and *Thema*. She is on the faculty of the brief-residency MFA in Writing Program at Spalding University, in Louisville, Kentucky. She also teaches in the Women's Studies Program at the University of Rhode Island, where she specializes in courses on feminist theory and postcolonial literature. Originally trained as an anthropologist, she received her PhD in English at Boston University, where she was a University Fellow. She also has an MFA in Writing from Vermont College. She has taught at Holy Cross, Tufts University, Harvard University, and Brown University. She now lives in Rhode Island.

The Fleur-de-Lis Press is named to celebrate the life
of Flora Lee Sims Jeter
(1901-1990)